Spies in Disguise

Kate Scott was born in London. She has lived in Hong Kong, Paris, Scotland and two tiny villages in France. She now lives in Dorset with her husband and two children. Kate writes children's books, children's television programmes, radio plays and poetry. She's had lots of different jobs but now she makes up stories – the best job in the world. She likes drawing, dancing, reading and watching films from the 1940s. She hates raw tomatoes and being tickled.

Spies in Disguise
Boy in Tights
Boy in a Tutu

Spies in Disguise

BOY IN HEELS

Kate Scott

Illustrated by Clare Elsom

First published in Great Britain in 2015 by Piccadilly Press
Northburgh House, 10 Northburgh Street, London EC1V 0AT

A CIP catalogue record for this book is
available from the British Library.

ISBN: 978-1-848-12417-2

1 3 5 7 9 10 8 6 4 2

Typeset in Candara 12.5/18 pt by Palimpsest Book Production Limited,
Falkirk, Stirlingshire
Printed and bound by Clays Ltd, St Ives Plc

www.piccadillypress.co.uk

Piccadilly Press is part of the Bonnier Publishing Group
www.bonnierpublishing.com

For Neil, co-founder of the PHF,
who turned January into June
(2,184 13ths and counting . . .)

Chapter 1

The good news: I'm on a spy-training mission and I have a bag full of uber-cool gadgets.

The bad news: I am in the women's underwear section of a department store and surrounded by BRAS.

I used to be Joe – until one day Mum and Dad told me they were spies who had to go on the run because their cover was blown. It meant a whole new life – new house, new school, new name. So far, so great – who wouldn't want parents with the excuse to drive too fast and use spy gear? But then they told me that to keep us from discovery, I had to go undercover – as a girl.

Yeah, exactly.

Not only do I have to dress as a girl, I have to dress as Dad's idea of a *girly* girl. He thinks it's only by having a completely over-the-top girl disguise that my real identity will stay a secret. Which is why I've been forced to wear ruffles, bows, sparkly hair clips in an assortment of animal shapes and way, way, WAY too much pink.

There are only two things that make me feel better about all this:

1. Sam – my one good friend since all this began. She lives a few doors away and goes to the same school as me. She loves football as much as I do and would *never* wear pink. She even likes my favourite fictional hero, Dan McGuire, who's a spy like us, except just in books.

2. Sam and I are being trained as professional

spies. We've already completed two spy missions – our first unofficial one, when we caught a teacher stealing school funds, and then an official operation when we stopped a dance teacher from pinching the contents of a football memorabilia exhibition. (That mission meant we had to take ballet lessons and put on tutus . . . I don't want to talk about it any more.)

Now we're on a training mission set up by my dad (which is probably how I've ended up surrounded by the *bras*). We've got to pick up a secret message and avoid being caught by an 'enemy spy' (Dad). Okay, it's not the best setting for an exciting spy mission but ever since my undercover life began, I've realised you have to work with what you've got.

I move away from a display of giant granny knickers and reach up to press the Ring-a-Ring spy phone clipped to my ear. It's one of our most useful bits of spy kit – a walkie-talkie disguised as an earring. 'Have you found it?'

'Yes, got it,' Sam's voice says. She's across the way in Textiles – we were assigned different departments to search and *of course* I was given the embarrassing one. Sometimes I wonder if my parents are out to get me.

'I'll meet you in Lighting,' I tell her.

'See you in five.'

I cut the connection off and turn to go – and find myself facing a smiling sales assistant. 'Do you need some help, dear?'

'Uh, no thanks,' I say.

The woman reaches out and pats me on the arm. 'I know it can be embarrassing when you're buying your very first bra. Why don't I select a few for you to try on? You could wait in the changing rooms and I could hand them in to you.' She gestures at the rack I'm standing next to. I flinch as I realise I'm right by the training bras. There's a sign next to them that says 'For the developing young lady'. For a second it feels like my feet are encased in cement, rooting me to the floor, even though my brain is screaming one word, over and over and over: RUN! RUN! *RUN!*

'How about this one with the little pink flowers

– it's ever such a pretty design.'
The woman plucks a hanger
with a pink strappy *thing*
hanging from it and dangles
it in front of me.

My face feels like it's been shoved in the
oven – I must look like a red pepper. 'No, really,
I'd better go – I'm meeting my mum,' I stutter,
backing away.

'All right, dear, but if you change your mind
about me helping, I'll be right here.' The woman
smiles at me kindly. You can tell she's thinking that
I'm too shy to let her help me and that I really do
want a bra.

What I *really* want is to take off this dress that's
covered with small yellow bananas and PUT MY
TROUSERS BACK ON.

I'm just about breathing normally when I get to
the safety of the second floor. To be extra careful,
I slip into the stairwell near the lifts, pull out a
raincoat from my rucksack and shrug it on over my
dress. Mum and Dad have trained us to change our

appearance as often as possible to lose anyone who might be tailing us. I step out into the nice, normal lamps and lampshades of the lighting department and breathe in the un-bra-tainted air. Sam walks up holding a four-pack of 50-watt light bulbs.

'What are those for?'

'I needed to look like I was shopping for something – that assistant over there was looking at me like I was planning a robbery. He must have seen me searching for the message.' Sam nods her head at a shop assistant standing next to a forest of standard lamps. He's staring at us with his eyes narrowed. 'I suppose it did look a bit suspicious, me lifting up every lamp.'

'Yeah, he's still watching us – let's go.' I take the light bulbs from Sam and walk a bit closer to the assistant. 'No, she didn't want these,' I say loudly. 'She said she'd already got them online. Don't you remember?'

Sam tucks away a smile before answering me equally loudly. 'Oh, that's right, I forgot! Stupid me!' She watches as I put the light bulbs back and then tugs on my sleeve. 'We'd better go meet her. You know how mad Mum gets when we're late.' We walk away towards the escalators at a quick pace.

'Do you think he's following us?' Sam says.

'Shhh!' I pull out some glasses from my bag. They're clear glass with tiny mirrors attached to the sides so I can see behind me. I can see the assistant looking after us but after a moment he shrugs and returns to the checkout. 'No, he's not following. But we'd better make sure no one else is.'

We make our way onto the escalators, going down to the first floor towards the café. As we get off at the bottom, Sam coughs twice – our signal to do the palm slip we've been practising for weeks. As she walks one pace ahead, she swings one hand behind her. I reach out and she presses the paper against my palm for a split second. In one quick move I clutch my fingers around it and tuck it away in the pocket of my dress (Dad finally listened to me about my need for pockets). Then I fake a sneeze, our signal to split up to confuse anyone who might be following us.

Checking there's no one around, I slip into the women's loos and find a cubicle to lock myself into. I take out the message and check it – it's in code, of course, and I don't have the cipher with me in case both message and cipher are stolen. Mum and Dad's top spying motto is 'Attention, attention, attention.' (Their motto is exactly as irritating as it sounds.) So I pull out my phone and take a photograph of the code, then send it to Mission Control at home. Then I tear the paper into tiny strips and flush them down the toilet. Before I leave I change into another dress I've packed in my bag, this one in bright red, and put on a matching beret pulled down low over my eyes. Finally, I empty out my bag and turn it inside out – it's a reversible rucksack with different colours on each side – before putting everything back. Mum and Dad have said that if you're being followed and you change your clothes for something more striking, then the person tailing you will often reject the possibility it could be you. Let's hope they're right, because apparently HQ think the results of our training missions are almost as important as our real ones.

Coming out of the toilets, I try to change my walk, hunching my shoulders forward, and tilting my head slightly to the side – but not too much in case I just look weird. There's a man wearing sunglasses and a large hat sitting right at the edge of the café, his face hidden by the newspaper he's reading. He glances up over the edge of his paper as I come out of the toilets. Trouble. I make a swift left and push through the door that leads to the main stairs and lifts. As soon as I'm out of sight of the man I run down one flight of stairs and go into the household goods department. I weave my way through the aisles of cereal bowls and the cooking tools that look like instruments of torture. As I duck behind a display of bone china mugs, I think of the best spy of all time, Dan McGuire. In *Dan McGuire and the Case of the Chipped China*, Dan McGuire has to run through a factory of four thousand china plates without breaking anything. Now I know how he felt. A tall woman in a hat is

cruising the aisles – she might be
looking for more than a
lemon squeezer. *Well,*
you're not going to squeeze
me, lady.

I bend down, pretending
to pick up something off the
bottom shelf and then stay
down as I scuttle into another
aisle and over to the doors on
the other side. I slip out and
then down the steps to the fire escape doors to
the street. I glance behind me. No one. I walk
quickly towards the meeting point Sam and I had
agreed upon – a café around the corner from the
department store. I see Sam waiting and, right
behind her, the enemy spy! I spin round and step
into the next doorway I see. I send her a text –
'Boring!' – our way of saying 'danger'. I wait for
sixty seconds and then peer out. The enemy spy is
gone and so is Sam – she must have followed our
back-up plan of returning to base separately. I hope

she manages to shake him off otherwise we'll fail our test.

I take three buses instead of one to be sure there's no one else tailing me. When I get home I go straight to Mission Control, Mum and Dad's secret spy office hidden behind a cupboard door in the kitchen. I tap the code into the panel to make the door slide open, and walk in. Mission Control is one of the best things about having spy parents. Some parents have a secret chocolate or crisp drawer. My mum and dad have a secret *spy room*. Every wall is covered with screens, panels with buttons and slots for gadgets, and the whole place is stuffed with more hi-tech gear than a James Bond film set. Mum and Sam are there along with the enemy spy – Dad.

'Well done!' Dad says. 'You passed that test with flying colours. HQ are really happy with how you're coming on, especially with your disguises.'

Mum holds up her phone, smiling. 'Yes, they were particularly impressed with the way you prevented anyone from stealing the code before it was deciphered. And you used a lot of other spy techniques too.'

'Change of location, change of appearance, change of accessories, quick message exchange, warning your partner about being followed,' Dad ticks everything off on his fingers. 'Really, it was textbook stuff, Josie.'

I wince at the name. Dad always tries to call me Josie, even when we're at home, so that none of us make a slip-up when we're in public. But it's like listening to nails down a chalkboard.

'Yeah, you were great,' said Sam. 'All I did was get followed by the "enemy" and almost be caught by that shop assistant!'

'That's not true,' I tell her, 'you're the one who found the code.'

'Admit it, the best spy won and that was you,' Sam says, grinning at me. 'But we do make a good team.'

'No. We make a *blinding* team,' I tell her.

It wasn't that long ago that it felt like Sam was better at *everything* than me. And okay, she's *still* better at football, but at least now I feel like we're equal as spies.

'We have some other good news for you too,' Dad says.

'We've got a new mission?' Sam and I have been hoping for a new mission from HQ for a few weeks now – we can't wait. The training exercises are fun, but it's not the same as the real thing.

Dad's smile gets wider. 'Well, yes, but that's not the good news I'm thinking of.' He scratches his stubbly chin and raises his eyebrow, clearly thinking he's 007.

He takes a breath to go on but before he can speak, Mum breaks in. 'You're going to be a boy again.'

Dad makes a grumpy *humph* sound. '*I* was going to say that!'

'You always take too long,' Mum says with a shrug.

'I don't care who says it – do you really mean it?' I switch my stare from one to the other for any signs that they're having me on.

Dad rushes to speak before Mum can say anything. 'Yes. As soon as the mission is finished, then we'll be moving on to somewhere you can be a boy. Though you might not be able to go back to being called Joe.'

'I don't care if I'm called Rumpelstiltskin if I don't have to wear dresses any more!' I can't stop smiling. This is the best news ever.

'We'll have to move quite far away,' Mum says, her expression turning serious.

'Fine, fine, let's move to Brazil! Anywhere! As long as I can be a boy again!'

And then I catch sight of Sam's face.

Oh.

'Ah,' Dad says, catching sight of our expressions. 'Yes, it's true that there's a downside to this.

Moving will mean we have to cut ties with everyone from our current life.'

So if I go back to being a boy that means no more missions together. No more best friend. No more Sam.

Why is it that every time Mum and Dad give me good news it turns out to be bad?

Chapter 2

Sam and I have agreed to concentrate on the mission first and think about what happens after it . . . later. As Sam said, 'We might as well enjoy ourselves while we can.' So when we have a Bangers and Mash meeting in Mission Control on Saturday morning, we're both excited. We've developed codes so that we can talk about spy stuff when we're out in public without anyone knowing. 'Bangers and mash' means a meeting about a spy mission. I *love* bangers and mash. Both kinds.

'So,' says Mum, gesturing to us to sit down. 'Your next mission is connected to mine. I need you to collect some packages containing extremely valuable items for me.'

'That doesn't sound very complicated.' I can't help feeling disappointed. Sam and I are used to planting spy equipment and following suspects, not just picking up a few packages!

'Just because it's straightforward doesn't mean there isn't an element of danger,' Mum says, shooting me one of her that's-quite-enough-from-you looks.

'Good.' I grin over at Sam – what good is a spy mission if there isn't a bit of danger? Sam grins back.

'Your mum's mission is a sting operation,' Dad says. 'Which is when you set out to catch an enemy in the act of doing something bad.'

'Like stealing?' Sam says.

'That's right,' Mum replies. 'But in this case we're

trying to catch an agent of ours who's sending our newest and most top-secret spy gadgets out to enemy spies.'

'Why would he do that if he's on our side?' I ask.

'He's a double agent,' Dad says. 'That means he's pretending to work for us while he's actually working for our enemies, giving them secret information about what we do and how we do it.'

'He's using Dan McGuire to do it too,' Mum adds.

I blink at her. 'Dan McGuire is a character in a book – how could *he* have anything to do with it?!'

'He's taking our spy gadgets and packaging them up in boxes of Dan McGuire merchandise so no one knows they're real,' Dad says. 'It makes it easier to smuggle the spy gadgets over to the enemy if they look like a delivery of toys.'

I'm speechless. How could anyone use Dan McGuire's name like that? That's like Father Christmas stealing sweets from kids! Or the Easter Bunny chucking eggs at chickens!

'So you're going to stop him,' I say to Mum. It comes out more like a command than a question but she must understand how I feel because she nods.

'Don't worry. I will.'

'Well, we're definitely going to do everything we can to help the mission,' I say. 'Right, Sam?'

'Right.' Sam is a big fan of the Dan McGuire books too, though she may not like them *quite* as much as I do (I bet she didn't have the last book pre-ordered one hundred and ninety-two days before publication). But she still likes him enough to look (almost) as shocked as I feel.

'The plan is to give the double agent some gadgets and make him believe that they're our newest and most top secret,' Mum says. 'The gadgets will be planted with specially designed micro-technology that will track where the gadgets are taken, record conversations, take photographs and send alerts back to HQ when they come into known enemy territory.'

'Will they be real gadgets or fake ones?' Sam asks.

'They'll perform a few spy functions to fool the

enemy spies into thinking they're the real thing but it won't be anything that involves our best technology,' Mum says.

'Basically the mission is to catch the double agent in the act and ensure the enemy spies don't uncover any more of our secrets,' Dad says.

'To make sure he takes the bait, I'll have to meet with him, giving him the primed gadgets – collected by you – so we can track them and prove that he's been sending them over to the enemy,' Mum goes on. 'Then, after that, I'll arrange a meeting so he can be caught by a special team from HQ.' Mum looks at me. 'You see, picking up these gadgets *is* extremely important work. HQ think the mission is less likely to be uncovered if you make the collections for me. You're in a perfect position to collect the packages in locations that won't be suspected, like your school, and you're also less likely to be noticed because of your age. But remember, Josie, you're to make sure that your identity remains a secret – being uncovered now would put the enemy spies back on our trail as well as ruining the mission.'

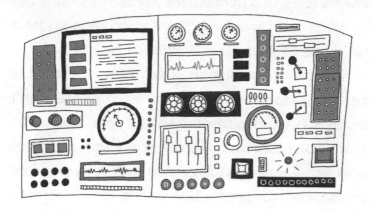

'Understood,' I say. As if I'm going to do anything to put my return to boydom in danger! I feel a lot more cheerful about this mission now I know there's a bit more to it. We're not playing postman, we're catching a double agent and protecting the good name of Dan McGuire!

'It sounds a bit dangerous for you though,' Sam says to Mum.

'You're right, Sam, it *is* dangerous,' Dad says. 'And that brings up something else.' Dad coughs. And I know that bad news is coming the way a footballer knows he's about to get a red card.

'*What?*' I narrow my eyes at him.

'Your mum will be doing this mission under a different cover from her current one. When she meets the double agent, she'll be pretending to be a spy-gear specialist from HQ. That way he'll believe he's discovering HQ's top secrets and won't suspect that she's a loyal spy trying to uncover him as a double,' Dad says. 'But it means she's going to need a body double. Someone to be seen going in and out of this house, maybe the odd trip to the shops in the car when she's out meeting the double agent. She mustn't be suspected as being a part of this mission under any circumstances. So we need someone to pretend to be her, here at home, in case there's any surveillance on us. It wouldn't be dangerous in the least.' Dad doesn't say anything else. He just looks at me.

It doesn't take me long to figure out what he means. 'No way!' I say at the same time as Mum says, 'Certainly not!'

But Dad's not listening to me – he's turned to

Mum. 'Zelia, we discussed this. You can't put yourself in that much danger without *some* protection.'

Mum laughs in a way that means she doesn't think it's funny. 'We discussed it and I told you that if I'm not prepared to have some random spy who probably doesn't even have her basic registration training impersonating me, I'm certainly not going to have Josie do it!'

It sounds like Mum thinks I wouldn't be up to being her double! Obviously I'd do it brilliantly if I wanted to – I just don't want to!

'I don't think you have a choice,' Dad tells her, in his very rare I'm-not-going-to-change-my-mind-about-this voice. 'And neither do you,' he says to me.

'It *would* stop your mum from being in danger,' Sam says.

Thanks, Sam. Make me feel *guilty* about not wanting to pretend to be my own mother.

'There's got to be another way,' I say.

'Of course there's another way,' Mum says. 'The idea is ridiculous.'

'No,' Dad tells us both, leaning forward. 'It would work. And it would mean you won't have a stranger in your house, Zelia. Besides, Joe's already shown how good he is at taking on a different cover and who could know your mannerisms better?'

Typical. I've been trying to prove to Mum and Dad that I have good spy skills and as soon as I've done it they land me into trouble.

'I'm not tall enough!' I protest. I've got to put a stop to this plan before it gets out of hand.

'You could wear high heels,' Sam says. 'You're not *that* much shorter than your mum.'

'Yes, it's a good thing you're petite, Zelia,' Dad says. 'That works nicely.'

'Why don't *you* do it?' I ask Sam. 'You're a girl – that gives you a head start.'

'But Sam doesn't live with us, Josie,' Dad points out. 'She couldn't be available at a moment's notice.'

'And my mum might notice if I kept disappearing,' Sam points out.

'I haven't got . . . you know . . .' I gesture at my chest. I don't even want to say it.

'Oh, a padded bra will take care of that.' Dad waves his hand in the air.

I stare at him. Mum also stares at him.

For once, my mum and I are in complete agreement.

'I suppose you're going to teach Josie how to drive as well, are you?' Mum says sharply.

'Don't be silly,' Dad says. 'I can do the driving when Josie's being your double.'

'She's not going to *be* my double,' Mum retorts.

'Yeah,' I say. 'It's hard enough being Josie, without being Josie's *mum* as well.'

'Anyway, it's time to give you the details of your first collection,' Mum says briskly. She keys in a few numbers on a Mission Control keypad and swivels to face us, shooting Dad one of her laser looks. I know what it means. It means *Drop the subject, Jed.*

'But –' Dad starts.

'The first collection,' Mum snaps. Her voice sounds like a crab clicking its claws.

Even Dad gets the hint. 'Yes, your first collection,' he says, hurrying over to the other side of the room, away from Mum.

They run us through the details and then Dad tells us we're free to go. We're heading off for a game of football when Dad calls after me.

'What shoe size are you again, Josie?'

I frown at him. 'Four and a half. Why?'

'Oh, nothing!' he says and waves me off, smiling.

I make a face at Mum that means Don't Let Him Get Any Ideas About the Body Double Thing.

She makes a face back at me that means Don't Worry, I Won't Even Consider It.

Or at least I hope that's what her expression means. Because there is NO WAY I'm going to agree to be my own mum.

Chapter 3

Mum seems to have had a word with Dad because he doesn't mention the whole body double thing at lunch. She must have made him realise how completely stupid and ridiculous and impossible the whole idea is. So when Sam and I set out to make our first collection at the post office depot that afternoon, I'm feeling quite cheerful.

The depot is behind the main post office in town.

It's basically a huge car park filled with all the Royal Mail vans that make the deliveries around the county. The instructions are to find the van with the licence plate details we've been given, use our set of spy car keys to open the van and pick up the package, which will have been marked with the HQ symbol.

Problem is, we weren't expecting quite so many vans.

'There must be fifty of them!' Sam scans the parking lot and frowns at the sea of red vehicles.

'We'd better hurry up and find the right one before someone notices us,' I say. 'I'll take the left side and you take the right.'

Sam nods and heads off. I walk carefully among the vans, keeping  a lookout for anyone working in the depot coming to ask us what we're doing. The licence plate number we're looking for is NE16 SSB and I read each plate off as I run from one van to another.

My phone vibrates in my pocket – Sam's found it! I run over to her. The van's parked right by the gates and she's already got the back open.

'You stand guard, I'll get in and grab the package,' she tells me, reaching up to pull herself inside. We've been told the package will be hidden behind a bag of emergency parts on the right hand side of the van.

Behind us, there's a bang as the depot door opens. 'Hurry up,' I hiss. 'I think someone might be coming!'

'I can't find the package!' Sam's voice comes out from the depths of the van sounding panicked. Sam's usually really calm so it makes me feel panicked too, especially when I see a driver approaching out of the corner of my eye. There's no time to get Sam out without him seeing her and asking awkward questions. Like what we're doing crawling about inside a Royal Mail van. My skin turns icy. We could blow the whole mission!

'Quick, hide!' I call through to Sam and then I close the van doors as quietly as I can. I crouch down behind the rear wheel and hold my breath, praying that the driver's heading to one of the vans on the other side of the car park so I can get Sam out quickly. But a second later I realise we're in trouble – the driver's door opens and shuts, and the van moves off! It's now I clock the licence plate – it's one letter wrong. Not only is Sam being driven off in a van, it's not even the van with the HQ package!

NE16 SSH

I leap up and pelt after it, shouting after the driver. 'Hey! Please! Stop!'

For a split second I think he hasn't heard me and then the van screeches to a halt by the gates to the road. The driver leans out of the window. 'What's up? What's happened?'

'I –' Time to think on my feet – fast. 'There was a cat – you nearly ran it over!'

'A cat?' The driver looks puzzled. I'm not surprised – there's obviously absolutely nothing in front of the van.

I hear the click of the rear doors behind me as Sam climbs out. I babble to cover the noise. 'Yeah, it was a big one, surprised you didn't see it. It was *huge*. Almost like a lion really. A lion cat! Like the musical. Except obviously the cat wasn't singing or anything. If it had been singing you would have noticed that, wouldn't you?'

The driver gives me a funny look, and leans back into his seat, further away from me, as if I smell. Maybe he thinks I'm dangerous. 'Yeah, well, it's gone now, hasn't it?'

I glance behind me and see Sam slipping back into the depot car park. 'Yeah, yeah, it definitely has. No more lion cats here! Thanks.' I step back and the driver revs the engine and takes off, giving me one last strange look before he screeches into the road and disappears.

'That was close!' Sam runs up to me. 'I didn't fancy being driven off on a postal round! Let alone coming up with an excuse of how I got in the van in the first place.'

'Yeah, it would have been quite hard to explain,' I say, grinning at her. My grin widens as I see over Sam's shoulder the van we're looking for, parked further back in the depot. Things are definitely improving.

Sam is frowning as she stares after the post van she got in, which is turning the corner at the top of the road. 'But what about the package?'

'I think we'll have more luck finding it this time,' I tell her, pointing out the licence plate I've just spotted.

Sam slaps her forehead. 'I got in the wrong van? Sorry! And thanks for stopping him from driving off with me. You covered really well.' She snorts. 'Though what exactly *is* a lion cat?'

I raise my eyebrows, pretending to be offended. 'Weren't you listening? It's an *enormous* cat that goes "miaow-*grrr*".' Sam snorts again and then we both collapse with laughter.

'It *did* work though,' I tell her when we've recovered.

'Yeah, it did,' Sam says. 'And it's hard coming up with something with no notice.'

It's good to know I can manage in situations like this now. I wasn't able to think on my feet like that when we first started working together.

This time everything goes smoothly. We open up the back of the van with our multi-remote key and Sam finds the bag within seconds. We're out of the depot in under two minutes with the package safely tucked away in my rucksack.

'Good teamwork,' Sam says, as we walk towards the bus stop.

'Bet none of the other spy partnerships at HQ work as well together,' I say. 'Except maybe Mum and Dad.'

'Yeah.' Sam sounds suddenly flat. I glance at her and see her face has clouded over.

My stomach sinks like a deflated rubber duck. I know what she's thinking. When we move, there will be no more working together. No more partnership. No more laughing about lion cats. More than anything, I want to ditch my girl disguise, but that doesn't mean I want to ditch my best friend too.

Chapter 4

When Sam and I come into school on Monday we find out a new boy is joining our class. Ms Hardy, the teacher who replaced Mr Caulfield after Sam and I proved he'd been stealing money from the school, brings him in after registration.

'Now, everyone,' she says, 'I want you to meet Curtis. He's new to the area and I'm sure he'll appreciate some friendly faces. You can all imagine how frightening your first day at a new school can be.'

He should try a first day at a new school pretending to be a girl when you're not. I bet my first day at this school was a *lot* more frightening than his.

While Ms Hardy smiles around the room, Curtis stands next to her looking at everyone as if we're a bowl of cold Brussels sprouts. If he wants people to be friendly, maybe he should start first.

Still, at the next break, Sam and I do our best to be nice. 'Fancy a game of penalties?' Sam asks him as we go outside.

'With a *girl*? I don't think so!' Curtis laughs, with a sneer on his face.

All of a sudden I go off the idea of being a friendly face. As far as I'm concerned, anyone who's rude to Sam is *not* going to be my friend. In any case, Curtis is stupid – why does he think that just because we're girls (well, one of us anyway) that we can't play?

Someone near us laughs – it's Noah. 'You should

try and play them, mate! They can beat anyone in the school,' he says to Curtis. 'Especially Sam.'

Sam flushes pink. 'Thanks, Noah.'

Noah shrugs. 'It's true.'

And it is. I used to feel a bit jealous about Sam being better at football than me but now I think her being so good is blinding. And it's not like I *never* beat her. It just doesn't happen every break.

Or every day.

Or every week.

I get into goal, shaking off Curtis's sneer, and concentrate on Sam. If you're going to have a hope of saving a strike on goal from Sam, you have to focus.

Not that focusing has ever actually helped me.

Sam swings her right foot back and wallops the ball. I fling myself up in the air to try and catch it but it skims the top of my hair and hits the back of the net.

Then she does it again.

And again.

And again.

It's not exactly *fun* to have Sam beating me at football but it's satisfying to watch Curtis's face crunch up with irritation when he sees how good Sam is. When we switch and I manage to get in five goals past Sam, he looks even more annoyed.

But when we pass him to go back into school, all he says is, 'Lucky.'

He's lucky Sam pinches my arm before I get the chance to say anything.

In the afternoon we find out that Curtis is good at a few things – like everything. He spends the whole morning sticking up his hand to tell Ms Hardy the answer – even when she hasn't asked anyone to. Even when the question is something like 'If Lesley has forty-two Wotsits and Ben has three and Sharia has eleven and a half, how many hours will it take before they buy themselves a family-size pack to share?'

But it's not him knowing stuff that annoys me, it's the way he seems to think that everyone else in the class is an idiot – especially the girls. In the last lesson before lunch, we're doing Ancient Egypt and he walks over to where Sam is working on her pyramid project.

'That's not bad,' he tells her.

'Oh. Thanks,' Sam says. She looks a bit startled, which isn't surprising because it's the first nice thing he's said since he started.

'Yeah,' Curtis says. 'I did something like that at my last school – when I was in Reception.' He smirks and moves back over to his seat before Sam can reply.

'Who does he think he is?!' I forget to keep my voice down and notice that Melissa and the rest of her girly girl gang look round.

'Shhh, boring,' Sam hisses, our code word for danger.

 The bell rings for break and Sam pulls me into the loos – the best place to have a quiet word (provided the rest of the girls in the class aren't having a mass meet-up, which happens a *lot* more often than I'd like).

'You've got to be more careful,' Sam tells me as soon as we've closed the door. 'Getting angry with Curtis could lead to you letting your cover slip.'

'How?' I reach up to touch my hair. My sparkly bunny hair clip is still in place. I look down – I'm still wearing tights and a skirt. I'm totally a girl. Sort of.

'You're supposed to be quiet and shy, the kind of person who stays in the background,' Sam reminds me. 'Getting annoyed with Curtis is going to draw attention to yourself. And you definitely don't want that.'

'Yeah, you're right.' I catch sight of myself in

the mirror over the sinks and flinch. Every time I see my reflection I remember how much I hate dressing as a girl. Particularly as this 'girly girl' Dad's forced me to be. Although it's hard to imagine being at a different school without Sam to joke around with, I still can't wait to stop having to dress like this. No more super-itchy tights, no more dyed hair, no more fruit-and-flower-patterned dresses. And no more *butterfly hair clips*. When I'm finally free, the first thing I'm going to do is put every single sparkly hair clip Dad's ever made me wear onto the floor and then STAMP on them with the largest pair of boots I can find until every single sparkle is crushed into DUST.

There aren't many things that can put me off my dinner, but the sight of my reflection with my dyed blonde hair teased into little stupid TUFTS all over my head would make the most delicious chocolate cake in the world look like a pile of mushy peas. And yeah, you guessed it, I *hate* mushy peas.

Sam's right – I can't afford to let Curtis get to me.

Chapter 5

At home it turns out I've got even more to worry about than Curtis. When I come into the kitchen, Mum and Dad are arguing and there's a line between Mum's eyebrows. I know that line – her stress levels are about to go from a banging-cupboard-door seven to full-on-furious ten.

'Zelia, you're putting yourself in too much

danger!' Dad sounds cross but I think he's actually frightened.

My stomach impersonates a yo-yo. What has Mum been doing and just how much trouble is she in? 'What's going on?' I ask.

Mum lets out her breath in a long whoosh. 'I had a bit of a narrow escape because someone was on my tail. I needed to lose them before getting into my new spy-gadget supplier disguise but I had trouble shaking them off even in the car. I came close to missing my meeting with the double agent to give him the first gadget you picked up – and that would have been a disaster. It looks like someone out there is watching me and that's not good.'

If Mum had trouble shaking an enemy off in the car then it's got to be serious – my mum is the fastest driver in the known world!

'You *have* to agree to it now,' Dad says softly.

Mum and Dad exchange looks and then Mum sighs a hurricane-force sigh. 'I know,' she says. 'But I still don't like it.' Her shoulders slump. All the anger's gone out of her. 'I'm sorry,' she tells me. 'I really am. But I'm afraid difficult covers sometimes go with the job of being a spy.'

It feels like someone's sliding an ice cube over my skin. I know what's coming.

I keep staring at Mum, willing her to tell Dad to forget it again. But her forehead's still all creased up. Which means . . . trouble.

'I can't,' I say.

'It's not like you'd have to do it for long periods,' Dad says. 'You'd only have to be in the disguise for about an hour at a time.'

Grown-ups are always doing that – trying to make you feel stupid for objecting to something because it's 'not for long'. They don't seem to understand that if something is embarrassing, the laws of time change and every second feels like an hour and every minute feels like ten years and every hour feels like *forever*.

'No,' I say.

Dad looks at me, his eyes all flinty. 'We need to make sure your mum's safe.'

It's weird when Dad gets stern. He looks all wrong – like a teddy bear pretending to be a shark.

'Josie, I wouldn't ask if I didn't have to,' Mum tells me. 'But this mission is even more dangerous than we first thought. If you can cover for me at home, it will help protect me.' The line between her eyes is now deep enough to plant a row of seeds in. She must be *really* worried. Suddenly I feel like I have to look after her instead of the other way around.

I take a deep breath.

'It doesn't look like I have much of a choice then, does it?' I say.

Mum hugs me. 'Thank you,' she whispers. 'And I really am sorry.'

'I know,' I tell her. 'It's okay.'

At least Mum knows what she's asking. Dad doesn't have a clue. Now that I've given in he's acting as if we're all on our way to a funfair.

'Good, good, good,' he says cheerfully. 'Don't worry, it won't be very different from pretending to be Josie.'

It won't be very different? It won't be VERY DIFFERENT?! Pretending to be a girl my own age is a piece of easy-bake *cake* compared to dressing up as my own mum. I thought wearing tights and a dress was horrendous, I thought wearing a tutu was appalling, but wearing *a padded bra* and *high heels*? What is *wrong* with him?

I swear to myself that when I am a real, grown-up spy, I will take revenge on him for all he's put me through. I'll make sure I get promoted so I can be

Dad's boss and then make him dress up as an orang-utan for a mission in London Zoo. He can eat bananas and pick fleas out of his ears for a week or two. Let's see how easy he thinks disguises are *then*.

'Right, well, you'll need to do your first mission as Mum in two days,' Dad says, unaware of my future plans for him. 'So be home straight after school tomorrow for training.'

'Two days? I can't learn how to walk in heels in two days!' I stare at Dad. He has got to be kidding.

'Sure you can,' Dad says. 'It'll be as easy as falling off a log.'

Falling is *exactly* what I'm worried about.

Chapter 6

Sam and I are on an early morning spy-training mission with Mum since I'll be doing the Training That Should Not Be Named after school. Mum texted Sam at six a.m. and then came into my room and ripped off my duvet – Sam definitely got the better wake-up call. It reminds me of *Dan McGuire and the Midnight Feast Burglar* – when Dan has to stay awake to catch a criminal who's stealing famous chefs'

recipes in the middle of the night. I bet he was almost as tired as I am. It doesn't help that apparently Mum's decided to train us in the art of goobledy-gook.

'First of all,' Mum says. 'I want you to learn a couple of cyphers so that you can code and de-code messages.' She pulls out a piece of paper with a double row of letters on it and shows it to us. The letters of the alphabet run along the first row, and then in reverse underneath. 'It's called the reverse alphabet cipher,' Mum says. 'If you want to write an "a" you write "z" and so on.'

'I see,' says Sam. 'And couldn't you make it harder by shifting the alphabet underneath further along? So "a" equals a letter in the middle of the alphabet instead of the last letter?'

'Exactly,' my Mum says, beaming at Sam.

I get it, but it makes my head hurt when people start talking about one letter meaning another. I like it when 'a' means 'a' and 'b' means 'b' or even 'b' means 'breakfast' or 'bread and butter' – I'm hungry.

'If there's any reason for a contact not to give you a package, you may get a message written in code about what to do next,' Mum goes on. She reaches into one of the gadget drawers and pulls out a slim black pen. 'Or, it could be written using this. An infra-red pen.'

'Is that like invisible ink?' This is more like it!

Mum takes a sheet of paper from another drawer and quickly scribbles something on it with the pen. She holds up the paper – it's still blank.

'Blinding!' I've always wanted to have some proper invisible ink. Before we went on the run, I did a lesson back at Bridleway Primary about using lemon or vinegar to write with but it didn't work out too well. First, because you could still see a trace of the message, and second, because Mr Burnside stopped the lesson when my old friend Eddie used vinegar to write 'Mr Burpslide'.

'So how do you find out what it says?' Sam leans in to get a closer look.

Mum pulls out what looks like a smartphone.

'An infra-red reader,' she tells us. 'You pass this over the sheet and . . .' She demonstrates and suddenly we can see what she's written – 'Bangers and Mash'.

'Why don't spies use that all the time instead of the code thing?' I don't see how reverse alphabet ciphers can compete with infra-red pens and readers.

'Because technology can be faulty,' Mum says. 'If you lose the pen or the reader, you have no way of passing on or reading your message, but with the cypher, all you need is a piece of paper and a pen.'

Maybe, but for me, an infra-red pen still beats the alphabet every day of the week.

'Just remember,' Mum says. 'If you want to communicate with each other about your mission, you must do it in code. For example, in one of my earliest missions it turned out that the postman was a plant – he wasn't delivering information, he was trying to collect it. Moles can pop up anywhere – but you know that.' Mum flashes me one of her laser looks.

Mum's talking about when I thought that a swimming instructor was a thief instead of a spy when Sam and I were stopping the football memorabilia exhibition being stolen.

'We'll be careful, don't worry,' Sam says quickly.

'Good,' Mum replies.

I flash Sam a grateful look. Mum's laser looks can make you feel pretty uncomfortable, especially this early in the morning.

'Now, the other thing you might need is a distraction,' Mum says. 'We've had a few new gadgets in from HQ which I think you'll find useful.'

She rummages around on the gadget shelves, muttering about Dad's lack of organisation, and pulls out a couple of small cardboard boxes. 'Here we go,' she says. 'The Scuttle Bug.' She holds out what looks like a small 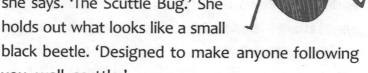 black beetle. 'Designed to make anyone following you, well, scuttle.'

'It looks like a Hexbug.' Sam peers closely at it,

making a face. 'Except this one looks *real*. It isn't, is it?'

'No, it's not real, but it is clever. Watch.' She sets the Scuttle Bug on the floor. The bug runs behind Mum's chair leg. A second later we hear some shouting, as if it's off in the distance. 'Follow me! They're over here!' and the sound of feet running along a pavement, getting louder and louder. There's a whistle and the noise increases – more feet, more shouting. Then the noise begins to lessen, as if the crowd is rounding another corner. The sound of running feet and shouts fades away into nothing.

Mum smiles. 'They are all individually programmable but they also come in three pre-set levels – use Level 1 to give the impression of a couple of people approaching, use Level 2 if you want a medium-sized crowd – that's what you just heard there – and Level 3 for a huge mob. It's very good at scaring off anyone following you – as long as they're worried about being noticed themselves. Which most enemy spies are.'

I decide that one of the first things Sam and I have to do is make a bunch of recordings – that is going to be serious fun. I reach out as she plucks another Scuttle Bug from the box and hands it over. 'Nice.'

'And then there's this.' Mum opens another box and pulls out a banana. 'Your dad's favourite.'

'Is this your weird way of making sure I eat more fruit?' I narrow my eyes at her.

Mum shakes her head. 'This isn't a piece of fruit you'd want to eat. It's called a Banana Slip.' She peels the skin down one side and throws it on the ground. Immediately a pool of liquid appears around it. 'That's chemically altered cooking oil, ten times slippier than almost any other liquid substance,' she says. 'You peel the activating skin, and as soon as the banana hits the ground the liquid is released and spreads up to three feet around it. If someone is chasing after you, even if they try to dodge the

banana, they'll still end up putting their foot in the oil and slipping up.'

I laugh. 'Brilliant!'

Mum holds out a cloth. 'Yeah, until you have to clean up the mess.'

'Wait – why do I have to clean it up, you're the one who threw it on the floor!'

Mum just looks at me and keeps holding the cloth until I take it. She's basically pulling the Grown-Up Card.

I'm telling you, you've never seen mess until you've seen a Banana Slip slick.

Once I've managed to get the oil off the floor, Mum gives us a set of ciphers, a couple of infra-red pens and readers and packs us off to school.

Sometimes being a spy can be quite hard work.

Chapter 7

At school, Curtis is apparently going for gold in the Olympics of The Nastiest Person On Earth. First he upsets Melissa before break by walking over to where she's sitting and making fun of her Hello Kitty ruler and pen set. He picks up one of the pencils and examines it, sniggering. 'How old are you, *five?*'

'There's nothing wrong with Hello Kitty,' Melissa says, her voice quivering.

The girly girl gang might not be my closest friends, and Melissa might be responsible for my having had to go to a pamper party when I first started at the school, which still gives me the hives whenever I remember it, but everyone knows Melissa doesn't deserve someone being mean to her.

Apart from Curtis.

'Of course there's nothing wrong with Hello Kitty. If you've said "*Goodbye Brain*,"' Curtis says. Then he laughs his nasty cheese-grater laugh.

Melissa sniffs and disappears out of the door with Suzy and Nerida as soon as the bell rings. I can hear them both telling Melissa to ignore him. Maybe it's because I'm used to thinking like a spy, but I can't help wondering *why* he's going out of his way to wind up every girl in the class.

But wondering about Curtis can't distract me from the dread of the afternoon – my first Mum Disguise session. Even Sam can't cheer me up.

'Think of it as the last leg of the race before you win,' she says.

'Someone usually overtakes me,' I tell her.

'Okay then, think of the next gadget training session,' she says.

I sigh. 'It's probably going to be something to do with dressing up as Mum.'

It's not always a good thing to be right.

The first thing Mum and Dad hand me is the Voice Over, a tiny gadget concealed in a necklace that nestles at the base of my throat.

'Why do I have to wear this?' I slide my finger under the necklace. 'It's really uncomfortable!'

'Hang on a second and I'll show you,' Dad says, his face lighting up with the same happy look he always gets when he's playing with spy gadgets. If Dad wasn't a spy, he'd probably be a gadget inventor. Dad fiddles with the clasp of the necklace and the pendant against my throat begins to warm up.

'It's not going to burn me, is it?' I say and then I go 'Ugghhhh!' because all of a sudden I sound EXACTLY LIKE MUM.

Mum shakes her head as if trying to get water out of her ears after a swim. 'I'll never get used to that. It's so strange hearing my voice coming out of someone else's mouth.'

'Tell me about it!' I say and then clap my hand over my mouth. Trying to *look* like Mum is one thing, but sounding like her is *way* too many kinds of weird.

Dad grins. 'You see, the Voice Over has been programmed to convert the sound waves of your voice to match the frequency of your mother's sound waves. Isn't it clever?'

Mum nods as I make another strangled sound – and even *that* sounds like Mum!

I really need to lie down in a dark room.

After some pleading, they let me take off the Voice Over for a bit. I tell them I can't concentrate with it on and even Mum admits it's distracting hearing me talk exactly like her.

'Your outfit awaits,' Dad says, pointing across the room. He sounds as if he's on the verge of laughing. I give him the dirtiest look I can manage as I drag myself over to the sofa and pick up a skirt and jacket. Underneath it is . . . a padded *bra*.

I stare at it. Maybe the heat of my hatred will be hot enough to make it spontaneously combust.

'Of course, my style isn't flowery so at least you don't have to wear a dress with little bits of fruit over it like you usually do,' Mum tells me, like this is a really good piece of news.

Oh, zip-a-dee-doo-dah.

 I pick up the bra with the tips of my fingers and hold it out at arm's length.

'For heaven's sakes, Josie, it's not going to *bite* you,' Mum says.

'How do *you* know?'

Mum raises her eyebrows so high they look like they're trying to jump off her face. 'Because I'm *wearing* one.'

'And that's supposed to make me feel better?'

Mum shakes her head and takes the *thing* from

me. Then she helps me put it on. It takes about an hour for her to teach me how to fasten it. Why do they have the hook on the back where you can hardly reach it? It's not like people have hands growing out of their backs! Finally, the *thing* is on. I pull on the narrow skirt, blouse and jacket and try not to look down at my chest.

'Not bad, not bad,' Dad says. 'It's good that you look so much like your mum.'

Fantastic. If I'd looked more like Dad maybe I wouldn't be standing here doing this.

Mum helps me with the red wig that matches her own hair, and then tells me to sit down so she can put on the heels. 'First of all, I want you to get used to the feel of them,' she says, slipping the first one on.

There's no way I'm going to get used to this. This isn't a shoe, it's a foot brace.

'My toes!' There's no possible way these can be

the right size – it's like someone's wrapped elastic bands round my feet!

'It's not that bad once you get used to it,' Mum says. 'Though actually I don't like wearing heels myself, hardly ever do.'

'Then why are you making *me* wear them?' I decide that she's going to join Dad in the Zoo Punishment.

'We have to get you to the right height somehow,' Dad says, shrugging apologetically as Mum pulls me to my feet.

'Arghh!' I fall forwards as soon as I'm upright. The shoes tip my whole body forward. Mum catches me and pushes me back into place.

'Take it nice and slowly,' Mum says, her mouth twitching.

Great. Now she thinks this is *funny*.

I breathe deeply, ignoring them both and take a step forward. Straight away, my right leg lurches to the side and I wobble on both heels.

Mum reaches out to steady me. She's not

smiling any more. 'Maybe this isn't such a good idea, Jed,' she says to Dad. 'I don't know if Josie can manage.'

'Nonsense,' Dad says. 'She just needs some practice.'

I take another step and fall into Mum's side.

'A lot of practice,' Dad adds.

By dinner time, my feet feel like they've been run over by an enormous truck. Mum and Dad only let me take the heels off when I've managed to walk across the living room three times in a row without falling over or wobbling. And I only managed that because I was holding my arms out to the side like a tightrope walker. Finally they let me take the heels off and I'm back to being myself. Well, myself dressed up as a girl.

'Tomorrow we master walking in heels – without the help of the arms,' Mum says.

'It's going to take ages,' I reply.

'It'd better not,' Dad tells me. 'We need you ready to be your mum by tomorrow.'

They can't expect me to manage heels that quickly! Anyway, my feet need time to recover – they feel like they've been attacked by an angry cook armed with a potato masher.

When I had to take ballet lessons during the holidays the pain was bad enough, but hobbling on heels is like specialised foot torture.

'It's very important for us to give the impression that your mum is here, doing ordinary things, to make sure she's covered when she's on her mission,' Dad says, his eyebrows knitting together. 'Do you understand?'

'Yeah, I get it.' Yet again I've got to make sure my parents are protected by pretending to be something I'm not. Who's the parent around here, anyway?

Oh yeah, *I* am.

I don't even get a break at dinner because Dad starts running me through all Mum's mannerisms.

'Okay, show me what your mother does when she's cross.'

I frown and jut out my jaw as far as it will go.

'I do not do that!' Mum says, frowning and jutting out her jaw as far as it will go.

Dad lifts his eyebrows up at me. 'If you say so, Zelia,' he says. 'Now show me what she does when she's concentrating on something,' he tells me.

I think for a minute and then lean over my dinner, frowning and poking my tongue out between my teeth.

'And I definitely do not do *that*,' Mum says, picking up the pepper and grinding it furiously over her food.

'You have to admit that you do frown a lot, Mum,' I say.

Mum's face crumples. 'You're making me sound horrible. As if I'm grumpy all the time.'

'No! Not horrible! Not grumpy! Just . . . you know, scary!'

'Thanks for clearing that up,' she says icily.

I realise I know another of her mannerisms.

When she's upset, her mouth goes really thin and she blinks a lot.

Way to go, Josie. Not only have I failed to be my mum properly, I've made the real one feel bad.

Chapter 8

The next morning, Sam and I get the details of our next collection from Mum and Dad. Now that I know how dangerous Mum's mission is, and how bad I made her feel last night, I'm determined to get everything right – even if it does make me turn a hundred shades of green every time I think of the Voice Over gadget and that *thing* I have to wear under my clothes for the Mum Disguise. The only thing I'm grateful for is that Sam hasn't seen me in them yet.

Dad picks up a black leather briefcase that's leaning against the wall, swings it onto the table in Mission Control and flicks the lock combination until it clicks open. 'The package will be waiting for you at the newsagent's around the corner from school, you can pick it up straight after your last lesson. Your contact will be a young woman with pink hair.'

'Pink hair?' Sam looks over at me and we make a face at each other. One of the things we have in common is that we both can't stand pink. Sam never wears it, but unfortunately for me, Dad decided it's a vital part of my 'girly girl' cover. I shudder as I remember that in my hair right this second there are *four* pink sequin hair clips, all in the shape of puppies. And the puppies are *smiling*.

'Yes,' Dad goes on. 'She's a spy whose cover is quite well, um, *loud* – and it actually seems to make her less suspicious. She's done a lot of undercover work for HQ. Anyway, when you see her, you need to tell her that your parents haven't received their magazines, *Patio Paradise* and *Celebrity Chatter*.'

Sam nods. 'Got it.'

'Then she'll say, "Oh, I'm sorry about that, let me see if I can find them." And then she'll bring out the package from under the counter.'

We wait but Dad doesn't say anything else.

'That's it?' I look from him to Mum.

'Yes, apart from you having to be quick because the shop shuts soon after school finishes, it should all be very straightforward,' Mum says. 'So hopefully you won't mess it up.'

'Excuse me! When have we messed things up?' A second later I wish I hadn't said it. I'm remembering a few things I slightly messed up. Like when I put my cover in danger by signing up to a swimming gala, or when I accidentally let Sam see my hairy ankles. Or when all the girls in my class got a glimpse of my boxer shorts.

Mum doesn't say anything, she just raises an eyebrow. My mum can say more with one eyebrow than most people can say with their whole face.

'It's good to have an easy mission for once,' Sam says. 'It takes the pressure off.' She grins at Dad and he grins back.

Sam's a good friend, so I'm going to forgive her for calling our mission easy. *Her* bit might be easy, but *mine* is definitely *not*.

'If anything does go wrong, don't take any chances,' Mum says. 'Play it safe.'

'Don't worry, we will,' I tell her. 'I'm too close to taking this skirt off for good to take any chances.'

It's true. I learned enough about taking risks during our last mission to want to try any this time.

Though what could go wrong with picking up a package from a newsagent's I don't know.

As soon as school's over, Sam and I make our way to the newsagent's. At first, everything goes to plan. I stand outside pretending to look at all the index card ads up in the window so that I can alert Sam to anyone coming in, while Sam checks to see if it's safe to get our package from our contact. Although we've got the coded cover story, Dad told us to pick it up when the shop is empty to be extra sure we're not being watched. While I stand there, a woman with a baby in a pushchair comes out. I pretend to examine an advert for a bike. Then Sam buzzes me on my earring phone – the Ring-a-Ring – to say the shop's empty. I'm about to give her the all clear to make contact with Pink Hair when I catch sight of someone behind me reflected in the window. 'Hang on,' I whisper to Sam and drop to my feet, pretending to redo the Velcro on my shoe.

'Hello, Josie.'

I glance up and catch sight of Curtis looking down at me. 'Oh. Hello,' I say flatly. I can't think of anyone else I'd rather not see. I finish fiddling with my shoe and stand up again.

'Waiting for someone?' Curtis says. He's staring at me like I'm going to crumble under his gaze – as if he's a policeman and I've been caught red-handed doing a robbery. What's his problem?

'Yeah,' I say. *Not that it's any business of yours,* I add in my head.

Curtis steps past me into the shop. I follow him. There's something odd about him appearing here at the same time as us. Even if it's nothing to worry about, I want to keep an eye on him, especially as he's been nasty to Sam.

Sam's standing in front of the rack of greetings cards, pretending to examine them.

'Buying a card for someone's birthday?' Curtis gives Sam a snaky smile.

'That's right,' Sam tells him. She doesn't give any sign of surprise that Curtis is there and that I'm not where I'm supposed to be, keeping a lookout outside. Sam's really good at keeping calm during missions.

She plucks one from the rack that's covered in pink rosebuds and says 'Happy Birthday to My Dear Darling' on it in gold lettering.

Curtis gives a half smile, half sneer and moves off to the magazine section.

I look over at the counter. A girl with pink hair peeks out from a door at the back and then disappears again. Our contact! I check my watch. We've only got two minutes left before the shop shuts! What are we supposed to do? I stare at Curtis's back, willing him to move, but he's picked up a *Dr Who* magazine and is slowly turning its pages. Maybe he's looking for pictures of his relatives – the Daleks. He's obviously not going to leave.

The owner of the shop appears and smiles at us. 'About to close, girls and boys. Make any purchases now, please.' Behind him I see Pink Hair. She catches my eye and shakes her head slightly.

'I need an eraser,' I say to Sam. 'But maybe I'll wait until tomorrow.'

'Eraser' is our code word for 'abort mission'.

'Okay,' Sam says.

As we leave, I glare at Curtis's back, as he puts the *Dr Who* magazine back on the shelf – very slowwwwwllly. I don't know why he's being so annoying.

But I've got a sneaking suspicion it's on purpose.

I follow Sam out of the shop. I wait until we're a safe distance away before I say anything. 'He's a real pain, isn't he?'

'Maybe he's lonely and he's trying to make friends,' Sam says.

I snort. 'He's got a funny way of showing it. And he's not exactly been nice to you, has he?'

'True,' Sam says. 'But maybe he's just jealous because I'm so brilliant?' She laughs but maybe she's right. I used to be jealous of Sam before I got over it. Maybe Curtis *is* jealous. Maybe there's nothing suspicious about him. I should give Curtis a break.

And I will – as long as he gives us a break first.

Chapter 9

When we get back and explain what happened –
how Pink Hair shook her head at us and how Curtis
was there, Mum and Dad go into Mission Control
and have some tense conversations in code. Then
they tell us that we'll be going back to the
newsagent first thing in the morning before school
– Pink Hair will open up.

'It's vital I get that package no later than

tomorrow,' Mum tells us. 'But to protect our profile HQ have insisted you two make all the collections so your dad and I can't pick it up ourselves. I'm going to have to meet the double agent this afternoon with a cover story – which will be tricky.'

Mum and Dad exchange a worried glance.

So much for me getting everything right. 'I'm sorry.'

Mum gets up and squeezes my shoulder, smiling. 'Don't worry about it. I'd rather you were careful than taking extra risks. Anyway, Pink Hair obviously felt it wasn't safe to hand the package over anyway and you must always go by the contact's instincts as well as your own.'

'Being a spy is about never trusting that things are as they seem,' Dad says. 'And making sure people can't guess what you're up to.'

Mum makes a face at me. 'Which also means that we need you to be my body double this evening while I'm out meeting the double agent.'

'*Today?*' I can't believe it. I've only had one session in heels!

'I know, it's not ideal,' Mum says grimly. 'But it's going to be hard enough to explain to the double agent why I haven't got the gadget I promised without worrying about being followed as well.'

'Don't worry,' Dad says. 'I promise I'll make the first trip easy.'

'You'll be fine,' Sam says. 'And just remember, soon you'll be a boy again and then all this will be behind you.' Sam laughs but then her smile disappears like it's been wiped off with a washcloth.

I know why because I feel the same way. This last mission already has as many yucky elements as the first two – but being able to be a spy with Sam has always made it worth it.

Almost worth it.

And soon I'll be gone.

After Sam's gone home, it's back to the heels and outfit torture. I get my Mum Disguise on, trying not to look at it, and then add the Voice Over.

I take one deep breath and then another. I have to keep reminding myself that I'm doing this to protect Mum – and that soon I'll be able to stuff every single part of this disguise in the bin.

We have another hour of me practising walking about in heels, this time with me trying not to hold my arms out like wings. I feel like an act at a circus, not like my mum!

By the end of the session, my feet have gone all red and squished, and I'm hobbling more than walking, but I'm managing not to fall over any more. Mum and Dad decide it's time to sit me down and run me through some 'Mum' conversation rules.

Mum checks her notebook. 'So when you like something you say it's –?'

'Blinding,' I finish.

Dad laughs. 'Um, no, definitely not a "Mum" word.'

Mum nods. 'If I like something, I say it's "great" or "very good" or, rarely, "excellent"'. She looks at me. 'In the *very* unlikely event that you have to speak as me – and your dad and I will be doing everything we can to avoid that situation – you must say as little as possible and only the kind of thing that I would say. Not anything that *you* would say.'

'You mean you want me to talk like a boring grown-up,' I say.

'A *very* boring grown-up,' Mum agrees.

'And be careful about the subject, too,' Dad says. 'No talking about Dan McGuire or what level you've got to on Mega Tank.'

'Stick to how bad or good the weather has been,' Mum says. 'Or make conversation about the person you're talking to. Say something nice about their suit, or their dress.'

'Oh, what a lovely cherry pattern you have on your blouse,' Dad says in a high voice. 'That kind of thing,' he says in his normal voice.

'For heaven's sakes, Jed,' Mum snaps. 'Undercover or not, I never talk like that.'

'But you want *me* to talk like that,' I say.

'No, I just don't want you to sound like *you*,' Mum says. 'This isn't a joke, Josie. If you *do* have to impersonate me at some point, you have got to be convincing.'

Suddenly Mum and Dad look more serious than I've ever seen them. I understand more than ever that:

1. Mum wouldn't be asking me to do this unless she really had to.

2. If I mess it up, she could be in huge trouble.

So if wearing shoes that turn my feet into strips of raw steak and putting people to sleep with my conversation about sunshine and rain and nice-looking suits is what it takes to keep Mum safe – I'll do it.

Chapter 10

Half an hour later, Dad tells me it's time to leave the house. Mum can sneak off once we've gone, after we've made anyone watching the house follow us instead of her.

I feel a bit sick. What if I mess it up and the enemy spies realise I'm not really my mum? What if I put her into even more danger? What if these high heels cut off the circulation in my feet and I'm never able to play football again?

At the door, Dad hands me a tiny pink tube.

'What's that?' I ask the question even though I know the answer because he *can't be serious.*

'Your mum doesn't wear much make-up but she does wear lip gloss,' Dad says. 'So you have to too.'

I stare at the pink tube in my hand.

'Come on, we need to get on the road,' Dad says. 'Your mum needs us to be seen out and about so that attention's drawn off her own trip.'

I take a deep breath and decide to count what I'm about to do as Mum's birthday present – for the next twenty years. I unscrew the cap and pull out the little stick with the sponge on the end that's covered with nasty, gloopy, pink goo. I raise it to my mouth and shudder as I smear it across my lips.

'Ew, it smells of *strawberries*!' I put the stick back in the tube as fast as I can and hand it back to my dad. 'It's disgusting.'

'What are you talking about?' Dad laughs. 'You love strawberries!'

'Not mashed up and slimed all over my mouth I don't,' I tell him.

Dad shakes his head. 'Here, put on the Voice Over, it's time to go.' He hands me the necklace.

I slip it around my neck, deciding that I'm going to be really, really quiet until this is over.

'And don't forget this,' Dad says, picking up a handbag like Mum's from the floor and dropping the lip gloss into it.

I forget my resolve not to speak. 'Do I *have* to carry that?' my mum's voice says.

Dad sighs. 'Look, Josie, I know this isn't fun for you, but it really is important.'

I nod. I know it's important.

It's also hideous.

* * *

It's one thing walking across a room in high heels. It's something else completely trying to do it outside. For one thing, our living room floor is completely flat but the path outside our house isn't. There are little holes and uneven stones everywhere. It's like trying to walk on stilts across a giant slice of Swiss cheese.

I can't believe grown-up women wear these things all the time! It should be against the law to put your feet in this much pain.

I manage to make it to the car without falling over by walking really, really slowly. I start to open the rear door when Dad clears his throat loudly. 'Ah, where are you going, Zelia?'

Oops. I forgot Mum doesn't sit in the back. I move round to the front passenger seat and get inside. The visor is down and I catch sight of my mouth in the mirror – *ugh*.

Dad starts the car. 'Just sit up straight and keep calm and this will go fine,' he says.

That's easy for him to say. He's not wearing a padded bra and toe-torturing heels. He hasn't got

Strawberry Eww Gunk all over his mouth. And he's not holding a HANDBAG.

Fifteen minutes later we pull up outside the supermarket.

'What are we stopping for? I thought we were just going to drive around a bit?'

Dad pulls at his ear. 'Um, yeah. Afraid there's been a change of plan.'

'*What* change?'

Dad jumps, as if it really is Mum speaking. I guess the Voice Over gadget has some uses. I can make Dad nervous by sounding like Mum when she's really cross!

'HQ want to make sure that if we are being watched, we keep the enemy spies off your mum's tail for as long as possible,' Dad says. 'So they wanted us to take our time about getting back and be seen doing unsuspicious things. Like shopping.'

Oh great. Not only have I been put into the universe's worst spy disguise ever, but now I have to hike around in these heels looking at vegetables.

'It'll be simple,' Dad says. 'We'll do a quick walk round the supermarket, buy some bread and milk and then we'll go home.'

'Quick' and 'walk' are not words that go together when you're wearing heels. In these things it's more like 'slow' and 'hobble'.

'Remember,' Dad goes on, 'Stay calm and try not to draw too much attention to yourself. We want to be noted, not noticed.'

'Right.' I've decided to keep to one-word answers as much as possible while I'm wearing the Voice Over. That should keep me out of trouble.

The tarmac covering the car park at least makes walking to the supermarket a bit easier than walking to the car at home was. But as soon as we're in through the doors, I have the opposite problem – the supermarket floor is so smooth it's like an ice rink!

As we're walking past the celery, my right foot makes a bid for freedom and slides forward. I reach out to grab something and clutch the first thing I reach – an onion. But the onion is at the bottom of the pile and now all the other onions decide they're coming along for the ride. There's kind of an onion avalanche.

So now I'm doing the semi-splits in a pile of escaped vegetables.

I think people might be noticing me.

But Dad's not a top trained spy for nothing. He swoops down with a trolley and puts my hands on top of the bar

'Go,' he hisses.

I use the trolley to get my balance back and steer a course through the onions.

Dad waves a supermarket assistant over as I move away. 'Sorry! I seem to have upset your lovely vegetable display. *Huge* apologies.'

The assistant looks a bit annoyed but comes over and starts picking up the onions.

'I'd help but my wife and I are on quite a tight schedule,' Dad says.

My wife – he means me!

I push faster with the trolley. The sooner we're

out of here and back home the better. I never thought I'd feel impatient to get back to being Josie, but being Mum is about a thousand times worse.

Dad catches up to me as I turn into the confectionary aisle. 'We definitely need to get you more walking practice,' he says quietly.

'I'm not going to have to do this a lot, am I?' I stop pushing the trolley. He's talking like this disguise is going to be *long-term*. There is no way I'm doing *this* on a regular basis!

'No, no,' Dad says quickly. 'But we can't afford any kind of drama when we do go out.'

'Sorry,' I tell him.

I can't help wondering if messing up my Mum Disguise will make HQ reconsider letting me go back to being a boy. I'm so stressed that I start reaching for a family-sized pack of my favourite chocolate.

'You don't like chocolate, *remember*, Zelia?' Dad puts

his hand on the bag and shoots me a warning look.

'Yes, but *Josie* does, *remember?*' I tell him, giving him my best impression of Mum's laser stare.

Dad takes his hand off the bag of chocolate. 'Oh yes, so she does.'

'I think Josie deserves a treat, don't you?' I say.

Dad nods slowly. 'Yes, okay then. As long as she doesn't overdo it.'

'She won't,' I say, putting the chocolate into the trolley. What does Dad expect? There has to be *some* kind of perk for putting me through this.

We manage to get round the rest of the aisles without me either:

1. Falling over

2. Making anything else fall over.

But at the checkout, there's a big stack of magazines and I completely forget who I am – or who I'm supposed to be.

'*Footballer's Weekly*! With a feature on Santos!' I grab the magazine and hold it out to Dad. 'Can I get it, Da–' I break off as I see the expression on Dad's face. I nearly called him 'Dad'! I'm supposed to be Mum! Quick, *think*!

'Uh, can I get it, dear? For Josie? You know how she *loves* Santos . . .'

Dad takes the magazine and puts it on the rack. 'I think Josie's had enough treats for one day, *dear*. We don't want her forgetting what she's supposed to be concentrating on, do we?'

'No,' I say. 'I guess not.'

Though there's not really much fear of me forgetting what I'm supposed to be concentrating on for more than a second when my feet are in AGONY.

We finally get back home without any more slip-ups and I'm out of the Mum Disguise in seconds. I flip the heels off my feet and wince over to the sofa, flinging the Voice Over down onto the cushions.

'Thank goodness that's off,' I say.

'Be careful not to break it,' Dad says, rushing over and picking up the Voice Over carefully as if it's a precious relic. 'Remember that you've got another stint as your mum tomorrow after school and you might have to speak. The disguise won't work if you sound like you.'

'I might sound like me anyway,' I say, thinking of how I'd nearly called him 'Dad' in the supermarket. 'I'm rubbish at being Mum.'

'Don't worry, you'll get better at it,' Dad says.

I'm not sure getting better at pretending to be my mum is one of my life goals.

Chapter 11

The next morning, I'm cursing Curtis under my breath big time. If it wasn't for him showing up and sticking around reading that *Dr Who* magazine, we'd have made this collection safely yesterday and I'd still be in bed dreaming of scoring the winning goal in the World Cup final. Instead, Dad yanks me out of bed at FIVE A.M. and sits me in front of a bowl of porridge and toast.

As if anyone's stomach wakes up that early!

Dad makes me eat it anyway, claiming that rumbling stomachs can be dangerous.

Yeah, if you're trying to creep up and surprise someone, maybe. But we're just trying to get to the newsagents while everyone else is still in bed.

Dad drops us two streets away from the shop. He tells us where he'll pick us up and warns us to be careful before he drives away. 'Remember, this mission is incredibly important – your mum *must* be able to deliver that package today if the double agent is going to believe her cover as a gadget specialist. We *have* to have that package.'

It turns out nerves are pretty good at waking you up. As we walk towards the shop, my stomach does a very good impression of a pot of boiling spaghetti.

'Looks clear so far,' whispers Sam.

As she speaks, I notice a movement in the shadows over by the bins. 'I'm not so sure,' I whisper back. 'Maybe set a Scuttle Bug Level 1?'

She sees where I'm gesturing and nods, slipping

her hand into her rucksack and pulling out one of the bugs Mum gave us. I cough to cover the sound of Sam throwing it to the ground. A second later, the murmur of two men having a loud conversation rings out from round the side of the shop.

'It's a great film, you must watch it,' says the Scuttle Bug. 'There's a scene where a boat turns into a helicopter.'

'Amazing!' the other Scuttle Bug voice says.

The shadow by the bins seems to melt away as the Scuttle Bug continues to make conversation about films and Sam and I head towards the door. Pink Hair is already waiting for us inside.

'Morning!' Pink Hair says. 'You girls are up nice and early!'

'My mum and dad didn't get their magazines, *Patio Paradise* and *Celebrity Chatter*,' I tell her.

Pink Hair glances round and then smiles at me. 'Righty-ho. I'll just get them for you. But hang on a sec, I think I've also got their bill from last month.'

Sam shoots me a look. This wasn't part of the plan. It must be a special message – I hope it doesn't mean trouble for Mum – or us. I take a breath, trying to stay calm. 'Okay.'

We follow Pink Hair and she slips behind the counter and ducks down under it, rising a second later to hand us a parcel wrapped in brown paper and an envelope. 'You make sure that bill gets to your mum and dad now, okay? Don't want them in trouble because  you forgot to deliver it, do you?' She looks into my eyes and I nod.

'Yeah, we will, of course,' I tell her, backing away. I stuff the envelope in my bag and Sam and I race for the meeting place with Dad.

In the safety of the car, I hand over Pink Hair's message. Dad rips the envelope open. 'Can I borrow your infra-red reader?'

I pull it out and hand it to him. Dad quickly scans the message with the reader, and frowns. 'Pink Hair has information that suggests that there might be another mole in the area trying to uncover a boy posing as a girl.'

Fantastic. A five a.m. start, followed by school, followed by foot torture and now a possible mole trying to uncover my cover. Could this day get any worse?

Football practice after school is one of the few things that takes my mind off my worries, though every time I pass the ball to Sam, I can't help wondering if playing football with anyone else will ever be this much fun. She's really good, but she doesn't make a big deal of it and she's always quick to shout something encouraging to other people on the team. And even though she's blinding at scoring goals, she doesn't hog the ball all the time but keeps passing it.

We're having a great game until, at half time, Curtis appears.

The boy is a fly. He's constantly buzzing up around you when you don't want him to. Which is always.

'Hi, Josie, hi, Sam,' he says. 'I thought I'd see

how good the *girls'* team is.' His lip lifts up into a sneer showing off his horrible little teeth. They look like rows of mini yellow Lego bricks.

Stay calm, I tell myself. *Be careful.* 'Well, you won't see much in half time. We're on our way to the toilets, aren't we, Sam?'

'That's right,' Sam says, her voice cool. 'But stick around for the second half. If you're very good we might even agree to give you a game some time.' She gives him her best little-innocent-girly-girl smile.

Curtis backs off. 'I don't think so,' he says.

Sam shrugs. 'Suit yourself. I don't blame you. Not everyone is up to playing us.'

We walk on, leaving Curtis behind.

'Nice one,' I tell Sam, grinning at her.

'So what's up?' Sam asks after we've pushed our way into the girls' loos and checked all the cubicles.

'Remember what my dad said this morning about there being a mole trying to uncover my Josie disguise?'

'Of course,' Sam says.

'I think it could be Curtis,' I tell her. 'He keeps trying to wind up all the girls in our class and I think he's doing it on purpose.'

Sam walks over to stick her head outside the door to make sure there's no one listening and then pulls back in. 'Yeah. He acts normally with the other boys, but it's like he's trying to make every girl in the class lose their temper.'

'I thought at first that maybe he just really hates girls,' I say, thinking of my old friend Eddie who didn't believe it was possible for boys to be friends with girls. It wasn't until I got to know Sam that I realised how wrong he was. 'But now that we know that there might be a mole around – and the way Curtis popped up in the shop . . .'

Sam nods. 'I think you're right. He *could* be the mole. He's new at school, and winding someone up is a good way to try and make someone drop their cover.'

'Exactly. People say and do things without thinking when they're angry.'

'Good thing you've kept your temper with him so far, then,' Sam says, grinning.

'Yeah,' I say, grinning back at her. 'But we'd better keep an eye on him from now on.'

'And *not* get wound up by him,' Sam says.

'Right,' I tell her.

Though that might be easier said than done.

'I guess we'd better get back,' Sam says. She pauses with her hand on the door. 'I'm going to miss working on missions with you, you know.'

I nod. Okay, so I'm going to miss having to come into the girls' loos about as much as you'd miss someone hitting you over and over on the head with a large hammer, but there's no getting round it, I *am* going to miss working with Sam.

Curtis is still on the sidelines when we get back but the whistle for the second half goes before he can say anything more to us. I try to avoid catching his eye as I run around the pitch but a couple of times I still catch him laughing when our side misses a shot at goal. Even knowing how important it is to keep my temper, it takes a lot of effort to stop myself from running over to push him face down into the mud.

After the match, Curtis walks up to us as we're gathering our stuff together.

'That was very entertaining,' he says. 'It reminded me of being at the circus.'

I clamp my mouth shut to stop myself from saying anything.

'Really?' Sam says. 'With you as one of the clowns?'

Curtis scowls and walks away, jamming his hands into his pockets with annoyance.

'Thanks,' I tell Sam. 'You stopped me from saying something that might have got me into trouble.'

Sam grins. 'Looking out for each other is what friends are for – right?'

'Right.'

And now I have an idea.

Chapter 12

'So if Curtis *is* a mole,' I say as we're walking from the bus stop towards home, 'then that's why he's been following us around. He's trying to see if the undercover girl will make a slip.'

'Yeah,' Sam says. 'But he can't be sure which one of us it is because he's been bothering *all* the girls. Though I noticed today that he wasn't paying much attention to Melissa any more.'

'And he did come along to football practice,' I say. 'That might mean he's suspicious of us. Or worse, suspicious of just me.'

'I don't think he's figured anything out yet,' Sam says. 'But we're going to have to make sure it stays that way by being extra careful.'

'Why don't we follow *him* to see if he really is a mole?' I suggest. If this is our last mission with each other I want to use all the spy knowledge we've learned together one last time.

A smile spreads across Sam's face. 'You mean do a proper surveillance mission on him?'

I nod, waiting for Sam to point out that we haven't been told to do it by my parents or HQ. Sam's great, but she does like to go by the rules.

But Sam nods. 'Yeah, okay, you're on.'

'Really?' My chest feels light with excitement, like it's been filled with helium.

Sam hitches her bag further up her shoulder. 'If this is going to be our last mission, then I want to make it count,' she says. 'Besides, you're right. Curtis is a pain.'

I might still have more Wearing Heels torture in front of me, and I might be getting closer to losing my best friend for good, but at least we're going to have some fun before we have to say goodbye.

Back at home, Dad tries to cheer me up about my next Mum Disguise outing by bringing me and Sam into Mission Control for another gadget training session.

It's hard not to feel better when Dad starts pulling out boxes from the gadget shelves. He's in his element, like Winnie-the-Pooh in a honey shop.

'Today is about making quick getaways,' Dad says, 'or hiding if a getaway isn't possible.'

This sounds promising. I exchange a grin with Sam as Dad hunts round for what he's looking for.

'Now this,' he says. 'I think you're going to like.' He holds up a small metal box. 'Ta-dah!'

'Ta-dah what?' I peer at it, looking for the flashing lights and remote control buttons.

Dad grins as he presses a hinge at the side and the box opens up and four wheels pop out. It's a skateboard! He places it on the floor. 'Hop on the ScootSkate.'

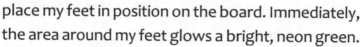

I get up from my chair and place my feet in position on the board. Immediately, the area around my feet glows a bright, neon green.

'Foot recognition software,' Dad says. 'Strong enough to be effective through shoes and socks. Remarkable technology.' He's got the same delighted grin he always wears when he's telling us about one of his favourite gadgets.

Before I can say anything, the skateboard makes a revving sound.

'Motorised!' Dad says. 'And fitted with GPS and steering sensors. Push down with your right foot to go forwards or backwards, and your left foot to brake. Steer by leaning the way you want to go,' Dad instructs.

'Okay . . .' I press down with my right toes and immediately the skateboard surges forward across the floor. 'Whoa!'

'Left heel to brake!' Dad shouts as I head towards one of the screens inset into the walls of Mission Control.

I lean back on my left heel and the skateboard comes to an abrupt stop, making me topple off it.

'That. Is. *Blinding*!' I tell Dad.

'Can I have a go?' Sam is already on her feet and hurrying over.

Dad grins. 'Got one especially for you, Sam.' He pulls out another skateboard.

For the next ten minutes, we take turns mastering the art of controlling the skateboards. Mission Control is big enough for us to skate round the corners of the room and we go fast enough to make Dad feel dizzy watching us. Eventually he waves at us to stop and sit down. We do, but I can't help keeping hold of the skateboard. I feel like Dad – in love with a spy gadget.

'Right, now we'll go through what to do if you haven't got time to get away, or you've left the skateboard somewhere,' Dad starts.

'I'd never leave this skateboard anywhere,' I interrupt.

Dad smiles. 'Yes, but say you're somewhere it isn't practical to use it, you might find this helpful.' He takes out what looks like a folded map and opens it up. It immediately becomes rigid, like a screen. Gripping it by each corner, he turns away from us and holds it out to the wall opposite. Then he turns the whole thing around and crouches down behind it.

'Wow,' says Sam. 'That is *really* impressive.'

She's right, it is. The screen has taken a photo of the wall opposite, so one side is now showing a picture of the wall. It makes the screen look as if it's disappeared – and Dad too.

'Brilliant, eh?' Dad says from behind the huge photo screen. He stands up, his hands outstretched. 'It's called the Spy Hide. It uses digital camera technology combined with the latest in malleable biodegradable plastics.'

'Right,' I say. I don't understand a word Dad's just said but he's happiest when he gets to go into detail. 'It's also a really cool bit of spy kit.'

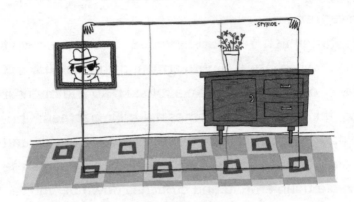

Dad takes out two folded Spy Hides and hands them to us. Then he checks his watch. 'Unfortunately, it's time for your other task today, Josie. Providing cover for your mum.'

The ScootSkate is blinding, the Spy Hide is great, but what I need is a gadget that gets me out of *this*.

As I put on the Mum Disguise I decide to be grateful that Mum's not the sort of woman who wears flowery dresses and lumpy cardigans. At least my mum has some dress sense.

You know things have got desperate when you're comforting yourself that you're putting on a more fashionable 'mum outfit'.

Once I'm ready, Dad tells me to get in the car. As we drive along, I keep remembering the way my foot slipped at the supermarket and the avalanche of onions. I've never liked food shopping much but now the idea of it doesn't fill me with boredom, but *terror*. By the time we turn off the main road, I've chewed all the strawberry goo off my mouth. Dad makes me put more of it on as we draw up in front of a low building with boxes of gravel in front of it.

'Where are we?' I peer out of the window at the dark green building.

'The local gardening centre,' Dad says. 'It's perfect. Mostly outside so not too much lighting, non-slippy floors and no vegetables piled in pyramids.' He winks at me. 'We'll just take a stroll around, maybe buy a packet of seeds and then head back. Your mum only needs long enough to hand over the package you picked up at the newsagents.'

My body floods with relief. Walking around a few green things should be a potato-planting doddle compared to shopping in a crowded supermarket.

We get out of the car and I manage to get across the gravel without falling over. There are plants in pots and people pushing around big trolleys filled with large bags and ceramic tubs and dozens of plastic trays with flowers in them. We pass a section full of rakes and little digging tools and a stack of wheelbarrows. Gardening looks like a lot of hard work to me.

'Let's have a look at the herbaceous borders, shall we?' Dad says loudly, for the benefit of anyone who could be watching us, I guess. I don't know what he's talking about but since I'm trying to keep speech to a minimum, I smile and nod as he leads the way. A woman near us is picking up one pot of green leaves and then setting it

down and examining another. I can't see what the difference is. Maybe she wants extra-big leaves.

Over in the corner, a man in a long coat and a hat pulled down low over his face is leaning against a shed and glancing our way. Something about him makes me nervous – is he following us? I nudge Dad as we pass a bank full of pots and give him a tiny nod to alert him. Dad gives me a waggle of his eyebrows to show he's understood and picks up one of the pots of flowers. I don't notice the little spikes on the stems and I accidentally touch one of them as he hands it to me.

'Ow!' Oops. The man by the shed perks up.

The woman who can't decide between two identical pots of green leaves stares at me. I smile at her, hoping to cover up, my eyes still on the man behind her. 'This one's got spiky bits,' I explain.

'Yes,' she says. 'It's a rose.'

'Uh-huh,' I say and then shut up when I see Dad shaking his head at me violently. I take a step back to get further away from the woman so that I don't say anything else that lands me in trouble.

And then I land in trouble.

The problem with taking a step backwards, on gravel, in heels, in a place that has millions of pots, rakes and wheelbarrows lying around is that it's very easy to fall over – into a pot, a rake and a wheelbarrow.

We don't say much on the way back home. As Dad keeps an eye on the rear view mirror and takes a long route to shake off Shed Man in case he's following us, he keeps muttering, 'It seemed a good idea at the time.' I slink down into my seat, replaying my fall over and over in my head. I'm supposed to *distract* attention, not attract it! I'm supposed to help Mum, not make things worse! Have I messed up the mission – and my chance of being a boy again?

Chapter 13

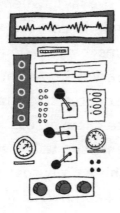

I think Dad's as worried as I am about the Wheelbarrow Disaster. The woman with the pots was nice about the falling-over incident and said it could happen to anyone but I still can't help thinking that I might have done some serious damage to Mum's cover. What if someone was watching us? What would they think?

Once Mum gets home, Dad pulls on his ear the

whole time he's telling her what happened, which is what he does when he's *really* nervous.

So when Mum just laughs, I know I'm not the only one in the room who's relieved.

'To be honest,' she says, 'when we moved here, I thought this might come up. So I decided "occasionally clumsy" would be a part of my new cover identity. Every now and then I trip up some stairs on purpose or drop something in the street. It can be useful to come across as clumsy. When you have an enemy spy tailing you they usually decide "ditzy" isn't a likely spy characteristic. So it won't have looked unusual if you were being watched.'

'Hang on,' I say. 'You "*thought this might come up*"?' I stare at her. 'I thought you didn't *want* me to be your body double? Now you're saying you thought one day your son might have to dress up as you, go out to a garden centre and trip up over a *rake*?'

Mum shrugs. 'Well, I didn't think of *exactly* this situation but working with your father I've learned that it's best to be prepared – for anything. Especially moments of embarrassment.'

As if she's had to cope with those! *I'm* the expert in embarrassment.

Dad starts to frown but then Mum laughs and he changes his mind and grins at her. 'Zelia, you are a marvel. As a wife, and as a spy.'

'You're absolutely right,' Mum tells him.

It turns out that Mum's second meeting with the double agent went brilliantly. She's sure now that he's bought her cover story of being the best contact for the most top-secret spy gear and she's told him to expect another two very important gadgets from her. Meanwhile, HQ have already started receiving intelligence that the first gadget she gave him is on its way into enemy territory.

'So now all we have to do,' Mum says cheerfully, 'is pick up the last gadgets, deliver them to him, and arrange the meeting where he can be caught by HQ and stopped from any more double-dealing.'

And, I add in my head, *prove that Curtis is a mole and stop him from uncovering my identity.*

It's about as easy as any of my missions – in other words, not very easy at all.

But nothing's ever stopped Dan McGuire, and nothing's going to stop me. Not even heels.

The next morning, Mum and Dad get me and Sam in for another before-school meeting in Mission Control to run over the details of our next collection. Sam's told her mum that we're doing extra football practice before class to prepare for a big game against another school. I still think I need to have a word with Mum and Dad about this whole early morning stuff. It's getting out of hand.

'Your contact will be at your school. His cover is as a temporary caretaker,' Mum says. 'That gives him the opportunity to be pretty much anywhere in the school we need him to be.'

'Okay, but what if people are around and watching?' Sam asks. 'Didn't you want to make sure no one could see when we made the collections?'

Mum shakes her head. 'These last pick-ups are urgent and have to be made as soon as possible.

HQ think that you two collecting the packages in school will be the safest way to do it. Although we think there may be a spy on my tail, they don't believe anyone is likely to be specifically watching you. As you know, their only worry is that there may be a mole somewhere in the area trying to spot a boy pretending to be a girl but they're not too concerned about that.'

'Why not?' I can't believe it. All this time they've been going on about how important it is to keep my cover and now HQ are saying they're not too concerned?!

Mum smiles. 'Actually, it's a compliment to you, Josie. You've been so good at maintaining your cover that they're confident you can keep it up until it's time for us to leave the area.'

Great. I'm good at being a girl. Just what I always wanted.

NOT.

'Of course, you shouldn't let your guard down,' Mum says. 'But be careful, as always, and everything will be fine. There's nothing to worry about.'

Grown-ups can't make their minds up – worry, don't worry, worry, don't worry.

I decide to worry a tiny bit – it's safer.

'Right, your next collection will take place at the school's Halloween party,' Dad says. 'The fancy dress makes it an excellent place to make a secret exchange without anyone being recognised or noticed. The contact will be there under cover as the caretaker, but at some point he'll change into a neon green-and-purple skeleton costume so that he'll blend in with everyone else but you can also spot him easily. And we're giving you particular costumes so he'll be able to identify you both too.'

'Good idea,' Sam says. 'And at least it gives Josie a break from dressing as a girl!'

I laugh. 'Yeah, I could use it.'

Mum reaches into a bag on the floor. 'Okay, Sam, you'll be a cat, and Josie, you'll be a pumpkin.' Mum pulls out a cat outfit, mask

and tail and what looks like a very large inflatable orange cushion.

'I'm going to be a pumpkin,' I say.

'Yes, Josie, a pumpkin,' Mum says. 'What's wrong with that?'

'I'm dressing up as a vegetable.' I shake my head and sigh. It's no use complaining, they'll never get it. 'Oh never mind, at least it's not a dress.'

'You'll be unrecognisable,' says Dad. 'That's the point. This costume covers your body and your head completely.'

'This costume could cover up the *school* completely,' I say. 'It's huge.'

Mum holds it up and examines it. 'Yes, it is a little on the large side but we don't have time to return it. Anyway, it's what the contact is expecting you to wear.'

'Fine,' I say. I guess after I've had to dress as my own mum, why should dressing as a vegetable bother me?

'Right,' Dad says. 'Now when you see the skeleton, the code phrase is "Cool costume."'

'Though obviously we say it to the skeleton, the skeleton won't say it to me,' I grin. 'Pumpkins aren't really "cool", are they?'

'That's enough!' Mum snaps. 'We know perfectly well how you feel about your disguise, and believe me, I wouldn't have you doing this if it wasn't important.'

'I was only joking!' But Mum's giving me one of her lightsaber looks and I realise this isn't really about the pumpkin costume. The thing is, I know that when my mum gets snappy like this, it's not always because she's cross, it's because she's feeling under pressure. And if my talented spy mum is feeling under pressure, I should probably be more than a tiny bit worried.

I don't say much after that, not even when Dad gives us both Click-It Rings that take digital

photos automatically when you wiggle your fingers. Because however cool the gadgets are, I can't help thinking that the work Mum's doing must be really, really dangerous if she's being that grumpy. And that means I need to do a better job at my part of the mission.

I'm going to have to be a better mum.

Chapter 14

When we get to school, trying to find out more about Curtis takes my mind off our most important gadget pick up. But finding out more about him is tricky. Curtis turns out to be as slippery as a Slush Puppie.

Sam tries to plant a tracker in his bag at morning break but it's almost impossible because he never seems to put it down. 'Bit suspicious, isn't it?' she says, as we stand to the side of the playground. 'Never letting his bag out of sight?'

'Yeah,' I say. 'And I think he's changed his tactics too.' I nod my head over to where Curtis is standing with Melissa and the rest of her girly girl gang. They're all wearing feathery things in their hair. From this distance they look like a herd of My Little Ponies. Curtis is talking with them and, instead of looking upset, they're laughing and nodding.

'He's trying to make friends instead of enemies now,' Sam says. 'That's not good.'

'Right.' I watch as Melissa chats away to Curtis – what is she telling him? She only has to mention the boxer short incident (when the top of my boxers were seen in the changing rooms and Sam had to invent a new fashion craze) for my secret to be out.

'Don't worry,' Sam says. 'We'll make sure we uncover him before he uncovers you.'

We'd better.

In the afternoon, Curtis asks to go to the loos. Five minutes after he comes back, the head of the school, Mrs Harrison, pops her head round the door.

'Ms Hardy? Curtis has had a call from his mum – she forgot he has a dentist appointment this afternoon. He's going to have to leave early – his mum will meet him by the school gates after lunch.'

Ms Hardy nods. 'That's fine. Thanks for letting me know. Curtis? Do you want to collect your things so you're ready?'

Curtis gets up with a smug smile on his face. There is no way that anyone smiles like that when they're on the way to the *dentist*. He must be up to something.

I quickly get out my infra-red pen and scribble a message to Sam.

'I forgot to give you your pencil sharpener back,' I say, pushing the note across to her, along with a pencil sharpener. 'Pencil sharpener' is our code for 'urgent message'.

'Thanks,' Sam says. Then she pushes the pencil sharpener off the desk. 'Oh dear, I've dropped it,' she says and ducks under the table. We've agreed to keep our infra-red readers in our pockets so that we can pass messages anywhere and not worry about them being read or found. When Sam reappears after a few seconds she nods at me – she's read my note and understood.

As soon as the bell goes we dash through the door after Curtis, who was the first one out.

It's time to get Eyes On Curtis underway.

Outside in the playground, we spot him talking to Evie. By walking slowly beside them, we hear him asking her how long she's played football, telling her that she's good in goal and generally reversing his approach from being nasty to sickly sweet. I nudge Sam. It's time for the Stumble and Slip plan. First I run towards Curtis, as if I'm on my way to see someone on the other side of the playground. Then I do the stumble – accidentally on purpose – that lands me (oops!) into Curtis's side, knocking us both to the ground. Sam rushes over to help pick us up and in the process slips a tracker into Curtis's bag.

'Sorry about that,' I say to Curtis. 'Are you all right?' I give him a Concerned and Caring Look but I don't know how convincing it is because he just glares at me.

'I'm fine,' he says, brushing himself down. 'Look where you're going next time.'

'Yeah, yeah, of course I will,' I say. I don't mention that I *was* looking where I was going – and I was right on target.

Sam and I both have the Sniffer Dog app on our phones from our last mission so now we'll know exactly where Curtis is at all times.

'It's good we managed that before the Halloween party tomorrow night,' Sam says, once we're safely in the toilets. 'Now if he *is* a mole, we can keep an eye on him.'

'And see if he's trying to keep an eye on *us*,' I say. 'Let's find out what he's up to now – because I don't think it's anything to do with the dentist. I'll use the Voice Over and call the school office.'

Sam grins. 'Go ahead – I've been dying to see it in action.'

'Keep a look-out though – the last thing we need is for Melissa to come in and hear me sounding like Mum!' While Sam opens the door a crack to peer through it, I dig down in my bag and bring out the Voice Over. I've been carrying it around ever since it dawned on me what I could use it for. I slip the necklace round my neck, pull out my phone and dial the school office. My heart thumps like a dog's tail as the phone rings. I remind myself that if I want to sound like my mum I'm going to have to *act* like her. I straighten up as the secretary answers and frown at the phone the way I can imagine my mum doing.

'Hello? This is Ms Marcus – Josie's mum – I mean mother,' I say, as sternly and confidently as I can. 'Josie and Sam have an important doctor's appointment today and will have to leave early – right now, in fact.'

'They have doctor's appointments at the same time?' The school secretary sounds confused.

'Yes, that's right,' I say, trying to make my voice clipped the way my mum does when she's in business mode. 'Sam's mother is writing an important article and asked me to take Sam to the doctor's with Josie.' I take a breath. 'I couldn't call before now because I've been on very important business, and as a journalist, Sam's mother is also obviously very, *very* busy.' I hold my breath.

Sam's staring at me in shock – I have to jerk my head at her to remind her to keep an eye on the door. I can't blame her. It's not often you hear your best friend sound exactly like their mother.

'Well, all right, I'll let their teacher know then,' the secretary says slowly.

There's a racket in the corridor – I can hear Melissa, Nerida and Suzy approaching. Sam jams her foot against the door so it can't be opened. She hisses through it. 'Toilet's broken.'

There's a babble of voices as Melissa and the others start asking questions. 'What's going on?' 'Are *all* the toilets broken?' 'I need a wee!'

'Uh, Ms Marcus? Are you near the school now? I can hear children . . . '

I snap to. 'Yes, that's right. I'm near the school. Very near. So that I can pick up the girls.'

'Oh, I see.'

'Right, I'd better go then. Please make sure they're ready straight away,' I gabble into the phone before I hang up and shove the Voice Over necklace back in my bag.

Sam steps away from the door and Melissa falls in through it. 'What's going on?' she says, looking around.

'Nothing,' Sam says. 'We thought the toilets weren't flushing but they're fine now.'

'Yeah,' I say. 'See?' I run into one of the cubicles and flush the toilet. 'Completely fine!'

Nerida stares at us. 'You two are really weird sometimes, you know that?'

You have no idea how weird, Nerida. No idea.

Curtis leaves straight after the bell goes for the end of lunch so he doesn't realise we're leaving school too and won't suspect we're on his tail. We follow at a safe distance, using the Sniffer Dog app to trace his movements.

Curtis is either not really the mole or else he's

not a very good spy because he doesn't use any of the skills Sam and I have been learning with my mum and dad. He doesn't backtrack or change his appearance or even look behind him! If he's training to be a real spy, whoever's teaching him is doing a rubbish job. I think of Mum and Dad and all they've taught me. They might have put me in the worst disguises known to spy-kind, but at least I know that they're teaching me the right skills to become a good spy.

Curtis heads to the leisure centre. We follow and watch him as he reaches the front doors and waits. We skirt the car park and hide behind a van parked in the road leading to the centre.

Sam pokes me in the ribs and whispers. 'Fancy a ballet lesson for old times' sake?'

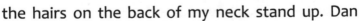

'Very funny.' Just the thought of the tutu I had to wear in our last mission makes the hairs on the back of my neck stand up. Dan

McGuire has been through some tough assignments – like when he had to get into a tank full of dangerous marine life in *Dan McGuire and the Pesky Piranhas* – but he never had to put on a dress or a tutu.

A black car draws up in front of Curtis and a man in a long coat gets out.

'That's the same man who was watching me and my dad at the garden centre!' I say, standing up and stepping forward to get a closer look.

'Do you think he's trying to find out about your mum's mission then?' Sam says.

'I don't know,' I say. 'Maybe they're trying to uncover me as a boy or maybe they're trying to uncover Mum as a spy – but either way we have to make sure they don't succeed.'

And right at that second, Curtis looks over in our direction. As I fling myself to the ground and roll away from the spot I was standing in I can't help remembering Mum and Dad's top spy motto – 'attention, attention, attention'. This is my fault because I wasn't paying any.

'I don't know if he saw me!' I hiss. 'We've got to get out of here – fast!'

Our last mission meant that we'd got to know the leisure centre inside and out and that comes in handy now. We slip round the building and in through one of the emergency exits to come out on the other side of the centre. I check the Sniffer Dog app.

'It's okay, he hasn't tried to follow us,' I tell Sam.

'Maybe he's getting instructions from that man,' Sam says, her eyebrows drawing together in a worried frown. 'But what if he *did* see you? I hope we haven't made things more dangerous for your mum.'

Yeah, me too.

We sneak to a position where we can see the front of the centre from a different angle. The man is still talking to Curtis and we see Curtis nod several times before they both get in the car. The car pulls away. We watch the tracker on our Sniffer Dog app as the car disappears round the bend.

'I guess that's as far as we're going to get today,' Sam says. 'But from what we've seen, it looks like we've definitely got to keep a watch on Curtis during the Halloween party.'

I nod, clicking on the Sniffer Dog app as the little blinking light shows the car getting further and further away.

The thing is, I don't want to just watch out for Curtis, I want to *catch* him out too.

Chapter 15

Sam and I spend the weekend preparing for the mission and playing football (except when Mum and Dad force me to do more Walking in Heels practice). The Halloween party is straight after school on Monday. As soon as the last bell goes everyone piles into the toilets to get changed. I look longingly over at the boys going into the *boys'* toilets before following Sam into the girls' toilets. One day soon,

I remind myself, I'll be able to go through the door with the little stick man on the front. One day soon, I won't have to panic every time I have to change for sports or a costume party. One day soon, dresses with fruit and flower patterns and sparkly animal hair clips will be washed from my memory like mud from a football kit after practice.

But for now, I'm stuck with the girly girl crowd of Melissa, Nerida and Suzy. They've apparently decided to keep the My Little Pony look. They still have the feathery things in their hair but now they've also put sheets around their middles and white shirts tied at the waist with ribbon. I have absolutely no idea what they're supposed to be. The ghosts of My Little Ponies?

Evie is pulling on a dark blue witch costume decorated with silver stars, complete with an enormous hat and a cloak that swishes. 'Like it?' she asks me.

'It's blinding,' I tell her.

Sam has put on her cat costume and comes up to me as she adjusts her tail. 'Let's hope they finish up soon,' Sam whispers. 'We want to get out there as quickly as we can.'

'Yeah, I know.' Eventually the ponies stop rearranging the feathers in their manes and the toilets are finally empty. I go into one of the cubicles, wiggle the bottom part of my costume over my clothes, pull on the pumpkin head and then press the little automatic 'inflate' button for the bit around my middle.

It inflates really well. Too well. In seconds, the costume has swelled to about a billion times its size. I am not just a pumpkin. I am a giant, PLANET-SIZED pumpkin.

And stuck in the toilets.

When I try to move out of the door, I get wedged in the door frame.

It turns out that you shouldn't really press the 'inflate' button until you're in a wide open space. A very wide open space.

'Um, Josie, why didn't you wait until you were out of the door to inflate it?' Sam says.

My vision through the pumpkin head isn't

brilliant but it's good enough to see that Sam is trying not to laugh.

'Stop it,' I tell her. 'This is serious.'

'Yes, yes, you're right,' Sam grins. 'It *is* serious. Seriously funny.' She collapses into giggles. When I keep glaring at her she takes a breath and gives one last little snort. 'Right,' she says. 'Where's the deflate button?'

'I don't know,' I say. 'But you need to find it!' I have one more go at pushing forward but it only means that I'm jammed even more firmly in the frame of the door.

'Okay, okay, keep your head on,' Sam says. Then she giggles again. 'Though that's kind of the problem, isn't it?'

'Ha ha. We do have something to do you know,' I tell her. I really don't want to have to tell HQ that I messed up one of Mum's most important missions because I got stuck in the toilet dressed as a giant pumpkin.

'Okay,' Sam says. 'I've found it.'

There's a hissing sound and the costume starts

to deflate a little. As soon as it's gone down to large continent size, instead of planet size, I push through the door.

'Hang on.' Sam fiddles with the button and the hissing stops. 'Right. You're all set. Let's go find that skeleton.'

'Thanks,' I tell her. 'You're a life-saver.'

'Well, more a pumpkin deflator,' Sam grins.

In the sports hall, everyone's gathered in their costumes. The walls have been covered in black cloth and there are – of course – little pumpkins hanging everywhere. The My Little Pony gang are already dancing to the music blaring out and most of the boys in our class are crowded around the table where the sandwiches, cakes and crisps have been laid out. I poke Sam in the arm and whisper in her ear. 'Have you checked where Curtis is?'

Sam nods. 'I tried to. But there's a problem.'

'What?'

'He put his bag down.' She holds up her phone with one hand and I see the flash of the tracker in the boys' toilets. The tracker dot isn't moving. 'He's probably put it in one of the lockers.'

It takes me a second to work out what she means and then I realise. We didn't plant the tracker on Curtis, we planted it in his bag. If he's put the bag down it means we don't know where he is.

And that could mean trouble.

'We've got to find our contact right away,' I say.

Sam nods. 'Let's go.'

We start walking round the hall, slowly. I scan every dark corner, figuring our contact will be keeping in the background.

'Wait! There he is!' Sam tugs at my arm and turns me around.

'Yes, I see him – let's go.'

We make our way over to the corner of the room where a neon green-and-purple skeleton is standing by a large plate of biscuits.

Sam opens her mouth, about to give the code phrase, when I catch sight of something behind her. I yank her arm and shake my head at her, making my pumpkin head bob about.

'Hey, Sam, it's a bit boring over here. Let's try over there,' I say.

Sam immediately nods and follows me to a spot in the hall where no one else is standing. 'What's wrong?'

'There's a problem,' I tell her. 'Curtis.'

Sam whips round. Curtis is over by the drinks, about three feet away from the skeleton. He's dressed as a Dalek (perfect costume choice, Curtis) – and he's looking our way.

'What are we going to do?' Sam looks from our skeleton contact back to Dalek Curtis. 'We can't make the collection if Curtis is watching,' Sam says. 'Then he'll *know* you're not what you seem to be. We need to get him away from the skeleton.'

'Okay – but how are we going to do that?'

Sam breaks into a smile as she looks at me. 'I think your costume is going to come in handy after all.'

It turns out that there are *some* benefits to wearing a pumpkin costume. Especially when it's been inflated to the max.

I move out into the middle of the hall and start to dance with Melissa and the other Little Ponies. I throw myself around to the music. People start to laugh and some of the boys join in. Noah pogos around the hall as if he's on a space hopper. I copy him, because let's face it, I pretty much *am* a space hopper. I dance closer and closer to Curtis, making sure I flail my arms as much as possible so that it looks like I'm completely out of control. Curtis edges away from me, towards the door on the opposite wall. Meanwhile, Sam is making her way over to the neon green skeleton. I see her speak and then take something from the skeleton out of the corner of my eye. When Curtis moves forward I do more bounce-and-flail dancing to keep him at a safe distance.

Which is a bit embarrassing when I realise the music has stopped.

Luckily everyone thinks I've been performing to make people laugh and I get a big round of applause. I do a mock bow and back away, waving to Curtis, who's now heading towards the door with a massive scowl on his face. Being a pumpkin isn't so bad after all.

Sam smiles as she comes up to me, pulling at her ear – our code for success.

This mission is definitely back on track.

Chapter 16

Waiting for the bus to school the next morning, Sam looks really serious.

'Are you all right?'

'I think we need to tell your mum and dad about Curtis.'

'I thought we agreed to investigate him by ourselves?' This is the last chance for me and Sam to work together – I wanted to have at least a bit of this mission in our control.

'But if he is definitely a mole and he's trying to uncover your disguise, then it could be dangerous – for you and your mum and dad,' Sam says. 'The mission isn't just about stopping someone from stealing something, is it? It's about someone giving away important information to enemy spies. He could make the whole thing fall apart if we don't manage to catch him before he catches us. I think we should tell your mum and dad everything we've found out so far.'

I hate it when people are right.

'Okay,' I tell her. 'We'll tell them after school. But until then, we put Curtis under extra surveillance.'

Sam smiles at me. 'Deal.'

Trying to watch someone in the classroom is pretty hard. Especially when you're supposed to be concentrating on a maths test. Luckily Curtis makes it easier by trying out his new Being Nice tactic on me and Sam. When Ms Hardy is out of the room, getting some more graph paper, Curtis walks up to our table and smiles. At least I think it's a smile. It could be that he's just put an entire lemon in his mouth and is wincing from the taste.

'Have you always been into football, Sam?' he says, leaning against the desk and twiddling with his watch.

'Uh, yeah,' Sam says.

I almost laugh when I realise that now Curtis seems to be concentrating on Sam! Maybe he thinks *Sam* is the undercover boy.

Curtis fiddles with his watch again. Something about that watch is nagging at me. It reminds me of something. And then it feels like a firework going off inside my head as I realise what it is. Finally we've got real evidence of what Curtis is up to.

I lift my hand and waggle my fingers as if I'm waving to Melissa on the other side of the room. She looks a bit confused (I'm not exactly a waving type of girl-boy) but I've got what I want – a photo of Curtis's watch.

Curtis has to go back to his desk then because

Ms Hardy comes back into the room but I'm grinning. If that photo shows what I suspect it will, then we have our proof that he's a mole.

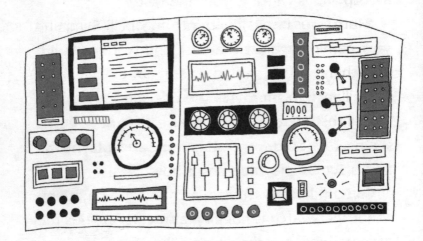

At home, back in Mission Control, I take off the Click-It Ring and ask Dad to bring up the photo on one of the screens. As soon as it appears, Mum swivels round to us. 'Where was that taken?'

'At school,' I say. 'We think a boy called Curtis might be a mole.'

'What?' Dad looks startled. 'You mean one of the kids in your class?'

'Yes,' Sam says. 'He's new and he's been acting oddly – trying to wind up the girls. We think he might be trying to make the person undercover slip up.'

Mum rakes her hair with her fingers. 'Why didn't you mention this earlier?'

I think about telling them about our little surveillance mission and then decide that maybe I'll tell them later – much later.

'We didn't have any hard evidence – until now.' I point at the photo on the screen. 'That is what I think it is, isn't it?'

Dad nods. 'Yes. Well done. You're absolutely right. It's standard spy kit. A recording watch. Even from here you can see the evidence of the micro NEBoo8.'

Whatever that is.

Dad strokes his chin. 'My guess is he's trying to record you talking. If you say anything suspicious then he can pass it back to his HQ. I assume you *didn't* say anything suspicious?' He looks sharply at me.

'Of course not!' What do they take me for?

Mum lets out a huffy sigh. 'I wish you would tell us these things straight away!' She turns to Dad, frowning. 'I don't know what we're going to do about tomorrow night, Jed.' The little line between her eyes is back.

'What's happening tomorrow night?'

Dad sighs. 'The last collection was supposed to be made during parents' evening,' he says. 'It's the most important gadget to pick up because it sets up the meeting where our HQ team will surround the double agent. But maybe doing the pick up at the parents' evening isn't such a good idea after all if this Curtis boy is a mole.'

Mum taps her fingers on the table by the gadget drawers. 'It *has* to happen tomorrow. I need that gadget. Maybe HQ can rearrange the location.'

I don't think I've ever seen Mum look this worried before. I reach out and touch her hand. 'Don't worry, Mum, we can get round Curtis, can't we, Sam?'

Sam nods. 'I really think we can.'

'We did all right with Mr Jones, remember?' I can't help reminding Mum of how Sam and I managed to convince the last enemy spy who tried to uncover my disguise that he was wrong.

'Yes, you did,' Mum says. 'And without telling us.' She narrows her eyes at me and then breaks into a smile. 'But it's true, you handled it well. Let's see what HQ say. Maybe they can find another place for us to make the collection so we don't have to worry about this Curtis kid.'

'Or maybe we can deal with him.' Managing to take this drop under his nose would be great. I'd like to pay him back for every nasty comment he's made – especially the ones to Sam.

'Did you say this is our last collection?' Sam asks. Her voice sounds really small all of a sudden, as if someone's turned her volume down.

'Yes, I'm afraid it is, Sam,' Mum says gently. 'It will be the last part of our mission here.'

'You mean after tomorrow night we'll be free to go? And I can be a boy again?' I can't believe it

– my trousers are finally in sight!

'That's right,' Dad says. 'But this is the trickiest mission of them all for your mum, which is why she's so worried. And why it's so important to take the drop without any problems.'

'I get it,' I say. And I do. I get it all – how dangerous this is, how good it will be for me if we get it right – and how bad it will be too. Because I'm looking at Sam and realising that this is our last mission together. Ever.

I might be about to get my trousers back but I'm also about to lose my best friend.

Chapter 17

Dad calls me for yet another pre-breakfast Bangers and Mash meeting. I really wish they'd realise that it's a lot easier to do important spy work when you've HAD ENOUGH SLEEP.

Sam's already in Mission Control when I walk in – she gives me a tired smile.

'HQ have decided that the drop should go

ahead,' Mum says. 'They're confident the two of you can handle Curtis.'

I grin at Sam and she grins back, both of us now fully awake – finally, we're being appreciated for our spy work!

'But there's another reason they want it to go ahead,' Dad says. 'And I don't want you to overreact to what I'm about to tell you,' he goes on.

Uh-oh.

Mum holds up her hands as if warding off a blow. 'I honestly didn't expect this.'

'It's only because it's so important,' Dad says, nodding.

'And once it's done, you'll be free,' Mum finishes up.

'WOULD YOU TELL ME WHAT YOU'RE TALKING ABOUT!'

Dad looks at Mum and, for once, she lets him say it. 'HQ need your mum to be in place for her meeting at the time you're collecting the last package,' he says. 'And it's vital she's not suspected of having any involvement in this mission – so we need you to be her body double one last time to distract attention away from what she's really doing.' He looks at me. 'We need you to be your mum at parents' evening.' He takes a breath. 'But we also need you to be Josie as well. It's essential the final collection is made by you *and* Sam to make sure it goes smoothly.'

'What do you mean, be Josie as well?' They can't be suggesting what I think they're suggesting. They can't. 'How can I be two people at once?'

'Obviously not at the same time,' Mum says. 'Just a brief appearance as one and then a brief appearance as the other. HQ think you and Sam will have a better chance of dealing with Curtis by working together,' Mum finishes up.

I stare at them. Since this whole by-the-way-we're-not-normal-parents-but-spies-on-the-run thing came up, they've made me dress as a girl, put on a tutu to take ballet lessons, and pretend to be my own mother. Now they're telling me I've got to be Josie and Mum on the SAME DAY?

'No, no, no, no, no.'

'We understand how you feel, honestly,' Mum starts.

'NO WAY.'

'It's for half an hour – max!' Dad says.

'NEVER.'

'It means you'll protect your mum and you'll get to be Joe again,' Sam says.

I look at Sam. She looks at me.

I *really* hate it when people are right.

Now that I've agreed to the Worst Mission Ever, Mum and Dad go into top gear. Mum tries to tell me all the words I can and can't say when I'm pretending to be her, while Dad tries to hand every gadget known to spy-kind to us. He gives Sam and me a pair of Cats' Eye Contacts each – contact lenses with in-built X-ray technology that makes it possible for you to see through up to three centimetres of any material.

'What do we need these for?'

'You have to take the drop to where your mum is,' Dad says. 'Because I'll be decoding the instructions to give her as the mission starts. These might come in useful.'

'Remember, if Curtis catches you, it could ruin everything,' Mum says.

Mum's a great spy, but she's not very good at encouraging confidence.

Sam doesn't say much on the bus to school and neither do I. Once we get through Mission Tricky I won't see Sam any more. But I'll also be able to be me again. It's like Sad meets Happy and they get into a fight where you can't tell who's winning.

And most of all I'm thinking, what if I mess this up?

Curtis seems to be staring at me and Sam all day. Any hope that he might suspect some of the other girls is gone. It's obvious that he's decided to focus – on us.

While we're working on our Egypt projects, Sam writes me a message in the reversed alphabet code:

YIRMT RG LM, NI NLOV. XZGXS FH RU BLF XZM.

Bring it on, Mr Mole. Catch us if you can.

After school, Mum and Dad make me rehearse the quick change I'm going to need to do, hopefully only once.

'Remember that it's all about the detail,' he says. 'One wrong element and –'

'Yeah, okay, I know,' I tell him. I don't need Dad making me feel worse – my stomach already feels like a bowl of waltzing worms.

After a few tries, I get the change down to two minutes and twenty seconds.

'I guess that will have to do,' Dad says.

What does he expect? Superman?

Everything's been timed and planned to the last second – Dad even makes us synchronise our watches. My fingers are shaking as I button up the top for my Mum Disguise and put the Voice Over around my throat.

'Ready?' Dad holds the door open.

'Ready,' I tell him, picking up the extra-large handbag that holds my Josie clothes. Sam's carrying her rucksack with the various gadgets we're going to need tonight. We've arranged with Sam's mum that Sam's going to come to the school with us and meet her mum there. Sam wears a hooded sweatshirt so that at a distance she can be mistaken for me and the three of us get into the car. Apart from one wobble on the heels as I open the car door, so far so good.

When we get to the school, I take a deep breath.

Dad turns to me. 'Remember, say *as little as possible.*'

'I *know*, Jed,' I say – and it is cool to see how Dad flinches when he hears my mum's voice telling him off.

Sam goes off to find her mum and Dad and I

walk into the school and make our way over to Ms Hardy.

MS. HARDY

She smiles at us. 'Hello – is Josie coming along tonight?'

'Oh yes,' Dad says. 'She's just gone to the loo.'

'Ah, right,' Ms Hardy says. 'Do you want to wait for her?'

You'd be waiting a long time, I think.

'No, no,' Dad says. 'That's all right.'

Ms Hardy smiles at me and I realise that I have to say *something* or she'll think I'm weird. Comment on clothes or the weather, I remember. 'What a lovely red dress,' I say. 'It goes perfectly with your eyes.'

Oops.

'Hahaha! Zelia has a bit of a sense of humour,' Dad says, at the same time as he nudges me sharply in the ribs.

I laugh. 'Yes, sorry! Just a little joke.'

Ms Hardy smiles, but in a thin-lipped, not very amused way. 'Yes, well. Now, Josie is doing quite well, though she does appear to be a little distracted at times.'

It takes a lot of effort not to glare at her. She should try having to dress as a girl when you're really a boy, and running missions as well as doing your homework. *She'd* be distracted too.

'Yes,' Dad says. 'Concentration is a bit of an issue with Josie.'

'I think she tries very hard, actually,' I say. I might have to pretend to be Mum but I don't see why I shouldn't speak up for myself. Or her. Or me being her. Or whoever I'm supposed to be.

Dad's phone bleeps. 'Sorry,' he says, 'it's a text from work.'

That's my cue. 'If you'll excuse me for a moment, I need to pop to the loo,' I say. 'But go ahead and look at Josie's work, Jed – I've seen it all already.'

'You have? I didn't think she'd taken any of it home.' Ms Hardy sorts through the folder in front of her, frowning.

Double oops.

Dad shakes his head at me so hard it might come off.

'Oh, I mean, Josie's talked so much about her school work that I *feel* like I've seen it,' I say quickly. 'She's very talented, you know,' I add. 'And very, very intelligent.'

Dad laughs his big, completely fake laugh. 'You would say that, Zelia, you're her mother.'

'Yes,' I say. 'But that doesn't mean it's not true.'

And then I walk across the school hall towards the toilets. I only slip once, just as I'm going in and then I'm inside the cubicle, ripping off the Voice Over, the heels and the wig and wiggling out of the jacket, skirt, blouse and bra. I stuff the clothes into the handbag, and shove it into one of the lockers, then I check my watch – two minutes and ten seconds. Take that, Dad.

I'm just about to go out of the toilets when Sam comes in.

'Uh, Josie? Aren't you forgetting something?' Sam points at my face.

Triple oops – I grab a piece of tissue and wipe off the repulsive lip gloss. I can't believe I forgot that!

'Ready to go?'

Sam nods and we exit the toilets, quickly checking around us.

'Time to start Mission Tricky,' whispers Sam.

'Let's make it a good one,' I whisper back.

We split up when we get to the hall. I go back over to where Dad is sitting with Ms Hardy. 'Josie! There you are!' Dad says. 'We thought we'd lost you!'

'Sorry,' I say.

'That's no problem,' Ms Hardy says. 'We were finishing up really. I was telling your father that you're doing very well overall.'

I think so too.

'I did want to talk to your mother for just one more minute, though,' Ms Hardy says.

'Won't I do?' Dad laughs but his knuckles turn white where he's holding his jacket – this wasn't in the plan!

Ms Hardy smiles. 'I'm afraid not. You see, I'd like to ask her about coming in to speak to the class about her career. I try to get a good mix of both mothers and fathers coming into the classroom.'

'Ah, right, I see.' Dad looks at me. 'Maybe you could go find your mother, Josie?' He checks his watch. 'I think she's got just enough time to come and have a word with Ms Hardy before we have to go.'

'I'll be right back,' I say.

I walk as quickly as I can back through the crowd of people that's built up. I almost knock Evie over on my way and she laughs. 'What's the rush, Josie?'

I think about telling her that I need to get changed back into my Mum Disguise as quickly as possible so that I don't miss the timing of the top-secret drop that's connected to my mum's mission. I'd quite like to see Evie's expression. But I don't, of course. 'I need the loo,' I say instead, and run past her.

As I'm about to go into the toilets I see Curtis coming towards me down the corridor.

This is *not* good – if he sees me go in to the loos as Josie and come out as my mum, he might put two and two together and come up with a 'spy in disguise'.

Suddenly our carefully constructed plan is falling apart.

Chapter 18

I reach up to my ear and press my Ring-a-Ring earring phone. 'This parents' evening is really *boring*,' I say.

There's a crackle but no answer – fantastic, my Ring-a-Ring has lost its signal. I don't even know if Sam heard me. Now what?!

I go into the toilets. Two minutes and five seconds later, I'm coming out of the cubicle as my mum. I even remember to put the disgusting lip gloss back on. I look in Mum's handbag to see what I've got in the way of helpful gadgets. It turns out Mum doesn't go *anywhere* without a few tucked away. I find a sound detector at the bottom of the bag and quickly stick it on the door – I'll be able to hear what's going on outside in the corridor.

Footsteps approach the door and then stop.

I break into a cold sweat. I think of my mum waiting for the package we need to take to her. I think of my dad, waiting with Ms Hardy. I think of my trousers, waiting in a future house where I can be a boy again.

My heart's pretending to be a drum kit and a pulse in my neck is beating against the Voice Over.

The door creaks open an inch and I take a step backwards. Curtis wouldn't come *into* the girls' toilets, would he? He's a boy! Okay, and I'm a boy too – but I'm dressed as a girl, I'm allowed!

Then Sam sticks her head around the door. 'Are you okay?'

I let out a breath and grab the sound detector, stuffing it back into Mum's handbag. 'I am now you're here – is Curtis still out there?'

Sam gestures for me to follow her into the corridor. 'I used one of those specially programmed Scuttle Bugs,' she says. 'The one we recorded to sound like a teacher. You know, the one that says she'll get the nearest kid to help clean up the sick on the floor. Seemed to work – I saw Curtis running back into the hall.' She grins at me.

'Good save,' I tell her. 'Thanks.'

'But aren't you supposed to be back to being Josie now?' Sam says, checking her watch. 'The contact should be here in less than ten minutes!'

'I know – I need to do one more thing and then I'm back,' I say.

'Good,' Sam says. She shakes her head. 'It's weird hearing your mum's voice when it's not really your mum,' Sam says.

Tell me about it.

Dad is standing by a wall, tapping his foot as Ms Hardy talks to some other parents nearby. I decide it's time to take this disguise seriously. It's time to *be* my mum.

I stride up to Ms Hardy, without even one wobble on the heels. 'Sorry to interrupt, Ms Hardy. My husband and I must be going now, but Josie said you wanted to speak to me?' I frown in my best imitation of my mum's do-you-mind-but-I'm-really-very-busy look.

'Oh, yes, yes, of course,' Ms Hardy says, flustered. She turns to the other parents. 'I'll only be a moment.'

I tilt my head and raise my eyebrows at her. 'Yes?' I check my watch. Six minutes.

'I was wondering if you might come in to our class to talk about your work. I understand you're an interior designer. I think the kids would love to hear about that.'

I bet they'd prefer to hear about Mum's *real* job.

But I start nodding. 'Yes, yes – I'm sure that's possible. I'll call you to arrange it in the next few days.'

If all goes well, we'll all be long gone in a few days.

Ms Hardy smiles. 'Thank you, thank you very much, Mrs Marcus, that's very kind.'

'Not at all,' I say, making my voice as crisp as toast. 'Now if you'll excuse me?' I turn to Dad and wave my hand at him. 'I think Josie is meeting us outside in a minute, shall we go?'

Dad grins. 'Absolutely.'

Once we've walked as far as the corridor, Dad turns to us. 'I'll see you in twenty minutes,' Dad says. 'You're sure you can do this?'

'Trust me,' I tell him.

Dad smiles. 'I do, Josie, I do.'

He walks away and I duck back into the toilets to whip back to my regular Josie disguise. Then I creep back into the hall where Sam's waiting for me. I check my watch – one minute to spare. 'Everything okay with your mum?'

'I told her I was coming back with you,' Sam said. She grins. 'It's not a lie.'

I look across the room and see our contact walking in through the door. I remember that in one of our training sessions, Dad told us you can tell someone to look in a particular direction without pointing by using the position of hands on the clock. 'The contact's at two o'clock,' I tell her. 'No, wait, it's more like one-thirty.'

Sam snorts. 'I'm not sure you've got the hang of the clock idea.'

I ignore her. 'What about Curtis? Do you see him?'

'Six o'clock,' she whispers. 'That means *behind you*,' she adds.

'All right, all right,' I say.

Sam hands me the crumpled piece of paper and while people mill around I walk up to the caretaker who's pushing a litter cart, ready with my code phrase. 'Can I put this in with the rubbish?'

The caretaker shrugs as if he scarcely notices me. 'Be my guest.'

But as I reach out to put the paper into the bin on wheels he's pushing, he nudges a tiny package that's resting on the lid forward with his hand. I palm it and then slip it into my skirt pocket. 'Thanks,' I say, as I turn away.

'No bother,' he replies.

Sam's already by the door. And Curtis is across the room, watching. Exactly where we want him.

Outside, Sam and I look at each other. It's going

to take all our training to do this right. Sam pulls out the extra rucksack she's hidden inside her own backpack and hands it to me. We get out the ScootSkates and hop on.

'Ready?'

Sam nods. 'Ready.'

We zoom forward along the pavement near the school, heading towards the estate. I look behind us and, sure enough, Curtis is after us – and he's wearing rollerblades. I press the Ring-a-Ring in my ear. 'Can you hear me?'

'Loud and clear,' Sam's voice says.

'Good – it's working again. Time for the banana.'

'Go for it!'

I pull out the Banana Slip from my bag, peel it and chuck it on the ground behind me. Then I press down with my right toe to make the skateboard zoom on.

When I look back, I'm just in time to see Curtis spinning in circles on the Banana Slip oil slick. He's pretty good on the rollerblades so he doesn't fall – but it's going to be a few minutes before he gets back on track.

We skate round into the large estate up ahead, weaving through the concrete pathways. When we get to the central green we stop and hop off, digging into our rucksacks and pulling out the Spy Hide. We shake out the material until it snaps into position, take a shot on the camera, then swivel the hide round and duck behind it.

A minute later, there's the sound of running feet – Curtis must have had to give up on the rollerblades. I've put in one of my Cats' Eye contacts and press my eye to the material of the Spy Hide,

CATS' EYE CONTACTS

being careful not to shake it. I see Curtis running up, then slowing to a halt as he looks around and sees us nowhere. He waits and then stamps his feet on the ground.

I've never seen anyone except toddlers stamp in a rage before. I have to clasp my hand over my mouth to stop the laugh from bubbling out.

Curtis the Toddler waits for another minute or two and then slowly moves off, checking over his shoulder every few seconds. We give it another five minutes after that and then move.

I switch on the Sniffer Dog app and see the two dots we need to keep an eye on – one is Curtis, moving further and further away, back towards school. The other is my mum.

*　*　*

The skateboards take us to her in no time. I flip the board up and fold it, shoving it deep into my rucksack. Then I take out the tiny package our caretaker contact gave me.

'Josie! Sam!' Mum's face breaks out into the widest grin I've seen on her face in a long time. 'You made it!'

'Of course,' I tell her. 'We're professionals.'

Mum reaches forward and pulls me into a hug. 'Well done,' she whispers. 'I'm proud of you.'

My face goes hot. Mum's not exactly big on saying things like that. It's a bit of a shock. A nice shock, but a shock.

'Now get out of here,' Mum says. 'I've got a mission to do.'

Now *that's* my mum talking.

Chapter 19

The next day at registration, Ms Hardy tells us that Curtis won't be returning to school due to 'personal problems'.

'Like the fact that he was a rubbish spy,' I whisper to Sam and she grins. I have a feeling Curtis is going to find it difficult to get any more spy work with the enemy HQ.

But all I'm concerned about now is my own

last day at school. Though no one except Sam knows it, after today I won't be coming back to Bothen Hill Primary. So at break and at lunchtime, I play as much football with Sam as we can fit in – soon she won't have the chance to beat me any more.

Mum's mission was a complete success – the double agent was caught and our gadgets proved that he'd been giving information to enemy spies for months. Dan McGuire's reputation has been protected. Mum's happy because she completed the mission and Dad's happy because Mum is safe. It all means that tomorrow I'll be on my way to a new life – a new life as a boy. I don't know where we're going, but I do know that if I ever see another pink sparkly bunny rabbit hair clip, it will be too soon.

I should be happy. Really, really happy.

But every time Sam slams another goal past me, I feel worse.

And it's not because she's winning.

* * *

We don't speak at all on the way home.

'Do you want to come in for a bit?' I ask her outside my house.

Sam shrugs. 'I don't know. Maybe we should just say goodbye here.'

'Oh. Right.' I stand looking at her. I can't think of what to say.

'Well – good luck with everything,' Sam says. 'I suppose you won't be allowed to have any contact with me in case they trace your new identity to your old one.'

I hadn't thought of that! I'd assumed we'd at least be able to FaceTime or text each other.

This is complete pants!

'It's been great hanging out with you,' Sam says, trying to smile. 'Thanks for all the missions.'

'Thanks, Sam,' I say. 'For – you know.'

'Not giving you away?'

I take a breath. I wouldn't have guessed it in a million years but having to be Josie did give me one good thing – Sam. 'For being my friend.'

Sam raises her hand in a half wave. She starts to

walk away towards her house. And I watch her go.

Then the door to our house flings open. 'Where do you think you're going, young lady?' Dad calls out after Sam.

'Let her go, Dad,' I say. I walk into the house feeling like a really, really flat tyre.

Inside, I slump down on the sofa and stare at the wall.

A minute later, Dad's back, clapping his hands together. 'I don't know, Josie, that's not a very nice way to treat your new neighbour.'

'She's our old neighbour, not our new neighbour,' I say.

'Um, not any more.'

I jerk my head up to see Sam standing next to Dad with a huge grin on her face.

Dad waves his hand at her. 'You tell him.'

'Are you sure?' Sam asks. 'But it's all down to you and Ms Marcus.'

'No, really, we think you should tell him.' Mum's appeared from the kitchen. She's wearing a huge grin as well.

'TELL ME WHAT?!'

Sam steps forward. 'HQ have arranged for a job transfer for my mum. What she's always wanted – a head journalist position!'

The excited feeling that had been bubbling in my chest dies down. A job transfer. That's all this is about.

'That's great, Sam, that's blinding news,' I say, because I know that Sam's mum being happy means Sam will be happy – and that's what you want your best friend to be.

'It's at a different paper to the one she works on now,' Sam goes on, her grin even wider. 'In the same town where some friends of ours are going to live. A really nice family – a couple and their son.'

'You mean?' I look from Sam to Dad to Mum and then back again. 'Us?'

'HQ think that you and Sam work really well together. They don't see why you shouldn't carry on working together – except from now on, you'll be back to being a boy,' Mum says.

I can't speak. I keep staring at them all, knowing that I'm grinning like an idiot.

I used to want to be Dan McGuire. But who needs to be Dan McGuire when you can be yourself?

FUN WITH CIPHERS!

Use your spy skills (and the ciphers in the charts on the opposite page) to decipher these messages and discover their hidden meanings. When you've finished, turn the page to check your answers.

1. First, see if you can work out what spy gadget is hidden here using the ALPHABET SHIFT +5 CIPHER:

YMJ ATNHJ TAJW

___ _____ ____

2. Now, using the REVERSE ALPHABET CIPHER, unscramble this message from Joe:

R SZGV UiROOB
KRMP WiVHHVH

_ ____ _____

____ _____

For your final challenge, decode this phrase – but like a true spy, first you'll need to work out which cipher to use ...

XUNJX NS INXLZNXJ

_ _ _ _ _   _ _   _ _ _ _ _ _ _ _

ALPHABET SHIFT + 5 CIPHER (or CAESAR CIPHER)

F	G	H	i	J	K	L	M	N	O	P	Q	R	S	T	U	V	W	X	Y	Z	A	B	C	D	E
A	B	C	D	E	F	G	H	i	J	K	L	M	N	O	P	Q	R	S	T	U	V	W	X	Y	Z

REVERSE ALPHABET CIPHER (or ATBASH CIPHER)

Z	Y	X	W	V	U	T	S	R	Q	P	O	N	M	L	K	J	i	H	G	F	E	D	C	B	A
A	B	C	D	E	F	G	H	i	J	K	L	M	N	O	P	Q	R	S	T	U	V	W	X	Y	Z

Create your own ciphers and have fun leaving secret notes for your friends (or to fool your enemies!)

There are lots of other codes to discover – you can use symbols or numbers too, the possibilities are endless!

ANSWERS:

1. THE VOICE OVER

2. i HATE FRiLLY PiNK DRESSES

3. SPiES iN DiSGUiSE

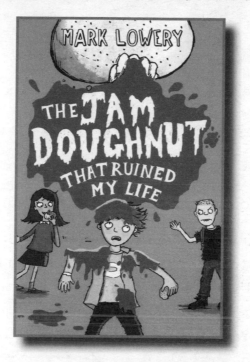

P R E S S

Thank you for choosing a Piccadilly Press book.

If you would like to know more about our authors, our books or if you'd just like to know what we're up to, you can find us online.

www.piccadillypress.co.uk

You can also find us on:

We hope to see you soon!